"Oh, Mr. Newcomb. You tricked me."

"I did nothing of the sort."

"Aye, you did. You brought us to a palace and promised every creaturely comfort. You won Duncan's allegiance by the promise of working with your animals, and my sister and her son will flourish instead of struggle. You said until Edward returned, you'd assume responsibility. I must have been a fool to think you changed your mind, but when you said that, I truly thought you'd reconsidered and were admitting Edward and Anna were wed."

"Now, Emily—"

"I was wrong to allow you to bring us here." Her voice shook, but he couldn't tell if it was with outrage or anguish. "Soon as Anna wakes, we'll go back—"

"No!" The word burst from him; then he cast a quick glance to be sure he'd not awakened Anna. He scowled back at Emily. "Look at her! You can't possibly last there another day. You're staying put."

She said in a sick hush, "You didn't tell us the cost of coming with you was Anna's dignity and our silence. You lured us here, but now you instruct us to live a lie."

"By staying silent, you're not living a lie, Emily. That marriage license is a fake."

CATHY MARIE HAKE is a Southern California native who loves her work as a nurse and Lamaze teacher. She and her husband have a daughter, a son, and a dog, so life is never dull or quiet. Cathy considers herself a sentimental packrat, collecting antiques and Hummel figurines. She otherwise keeps busy with reading, writing, baking, and being a prayer warrior. "I am easily distracted during prayer, so I devote certain tasks and chores to specific requests or persons so I can keep faithful in my prayer life."

Books by Cathy Marie Hake

HEARTSONG PRESENTS
HP370—Twin Victories
HP481—Unexpected Delivery

Precious
Burdens

Cathy Marie Hake

Heartsong Presents

A note from the author:
I love to hear from my readers! You may correspond with me by writing:

Cathy Marie Hake
Author Relations
PO Box 719
Uhrichsville, OH 44683

ISBN 1-58660-626-3

PRECIOUS BURDENS

All Scripture quotations are taken from the King James Version of the Bible.

All of the characters and events in this book are fictitious. Any resemblance to actual persons, living or dead, or to actual events is purely coincidental.

Cover illustration by Dick Bobnick.

PRINTED IN THE U.S.A.

one

Virginia, 1846

"God sends meat; the devil brings cookies." Emily O'Brien interjected a lighthearted tone into her voice, even though she truly wished she could afford an occasional treat for her six-year-old brother. She turned away so he couldn't see her sadness, grabbed the nearly empty bottle, and poured a cup of watered-down milk for him.

"Emily," Duncan asked plaintively, "do you suppose it would be terrible bad if we invited the devil in just long enough to get a few cookies?"

"Ach! Now what kind of talk is that?" She turned back around in the cramped space between the food shelf and the table, set the tin mug down before him, and ruffled his red curls. "You're a good lad, Duncan. You'd never want to do business with that pitchfork-carryin' demon."

"Aye, right you are."

A tiny bleat of sound distracted Duncan's attention. He glanced over at the bed where their sister and her newborn lay, then lowered his voice to a bare whisper. "Our Em, what are you going to do?"

His innocent question nearly broke her heart. His childlike belief that she could handle this made her breath hitch. Emily forced a smile. "I'll go check on things today."

Emily pulled the thin curtains over the window, then smoothed the skirt of her mud brown serge dress and tugged her shawl tighter. "You know what to do, Duncan-mine. I'll be back quick as I can."

Emily left the one-room shack and waited until she heard the latch slide home before she started toward the docks. Hopefully, when she returned, she'd not be alone. They'd been faithful to pray for Anna's husband each and every day of his voyage. Mayhap the *Cormorant* had docked while Anna labored, and news just hadn't come yet. As the captain, Edward would be busy when he docked his fine vessel.

He has to be home. What am I to do if he's not? Duncan and Anna are starving, and the babe won't stay healthy if we've no coal. The midwife's still wanting her money, and rent is due. If he's not here yet, maybe I can at least get word on when the ship is due in.

Another blast of cold air swept by, causing Emily to cease her musing. Huddled beneath her shawl, she scurried to get out of the harsh wind. "Dear Lord in heaven," she prayed under her breath, "if You could see clear to helpin' Edward be home with enough jingling in his pocket to keep us from being so cold and hungry, I'd count it as a real blessing."

❧

"I'm looking for Edward Newcomb." Emily shivered as much from fear as cold while she stood at the bay side and made her inquiries. A more dangerous place didn't exist. Rough sailors passed by and treated her like a brazen hussy for asking about a man. No woman of decency came down here, but she had no choice. Desperation drove her. The men leered at her. One made comments saltier than the ocean air and grabbed for her. She hastily stepped backward, tripped, and fell over a coil of thick, hemp ropes. A small cry curled in her throat as a haze of red engulfed her.

"Hey! Enough of that!" A tall, beautifully dressed gentleman strode up a narrow gangplank, along the sea-splashed dock, and crossed over toward her. The riffraff scuttled away like bilge rats in a storm. "Here now, Miss. This isn't a safe place. You'd best get along home."

"Thank you," Emily said as he lifted her from the damp ground. The moment he set her back on her feet, she compressed her lips against the fiery pain that shot up from her left ankle.

He made no move to leave. Since he stood with his back to the sun, she couldn't see his shadowed face; but a kind tone urged, "You'd best go now, Miss. This is no place for you."

For the first time since she'd set foot here, she felt safe. This man radiated authority and strength. Of all people, he could probably give her the best information. "Sir, I need help. I'm looking for someone."

He looked at her for a long moment, assessing her. Gulls cried, sails luffed, and the ropes mooring ships to the dock creaked. All around them, the bustle of dock life continued; but everything seemed motionless right here, and Emily fought not to squirm under this strange man's silent scrutiny. The fact that she couldn't clearly see his features made the whole situation feel even more awkward. She blurted out, "My sister's husband has been at sea for almost eight months, and I need news of his ship."

His voice softened with sympathy. "Well, then, let's get you some answers. Franklin!" The gentleman must have noticed her squinting into the rising sun. He stepped to the side so she could pivot. Finally she saw more of him than a mere silhouette. Dark brown, waving hair, heavy brows over deep-set, tea-colored eyes, and a strong, square chin. For a moment Emily almost gasped at how familiar he looked—but, no, that was merely a trick of the morning light. He was taller, broader, and far more handsome than Edward. She chided herself for being so fanciful when she needed to locate her sister's husband at once.

A portly man bustled up. "Aye, Sir?"

"Franklin, this lady needs our assistance," the gentleman said. "Her brother-in-law's ship, the—" He turned and looked at her.

"The *Cormorant*," she supplied.

The men exchanged a telling look. Emily's heart skipped a beat. The gentleman discreetly leaned a little closer and lowered his voice confidentially. "Miss, the *Cormorant* came home and set voyage the last week in May." Pity stole over his face as he added, "And she just set sail again yesterday."

Emily felt the blood drain from her face. She stared at him and shook her head. "No." She swallowed hard and tried to mind her manners while grasping for one last hope. "Mayhap that was another *Cormorant*, Sir. He wed my sister. Right and tight he did. Anna had the babe two nights ago. She's ailing bad."

The gentleman shifted his weight so the sun now struck features that carried a reassuring mixture of compassion and concern. "I'll see to it the sailor meets his obligations," he promised in a voice as reliable as iron. "What is his name?"

"His name is Edward, Sir. Edward Newcomb."

The gentleman's eyes narrowed, and his face grew unrelenting and harsh as a blizzard. "Begone, Wench. I'll not be taken in by such a tale."

" 'Tis the honest truth!"

"You wouldn't know the truth if it were served to you on a china supper plate." His voice went cold as sleet. "Edward Newcomb is my brother. I, of all people, would know if he were married. Now leave."

Emily stared at him in disbelief.

"Away with you. I'll not stand by and allow anyone to slander my brother's reputation or dishonor our family name with such an outrageous fabrication."

A wave of anger overtook her horror. "Fabrication?! He's married, he is. He's a father now, too. You tell him Anna gave him a son." Pride aching, she straightened her shoulders. "You tell your brother that while he's been larking around, his wife's dinner plate was empty. That, Mr. Newcomb, is the truth—and you can just choke on your fancy china and lies!"

Back straight as a rod, Emily turned to walk off. She bit her lower lip against the throbbing in her ankle and hobbled faster. Each step hurt worse than the last. She wasn't going to show it, though. She managed to get clear past the docks and to the street before she couldn't bear to go farther. There she leaned against the trunk of a wind-twisted tree and closed her eyes in anguish.

What am I going to tell Anna?

&

John Newcomb watched the dignified woman limp off. Even dressed in what looked like a prim nanny's ragged castoffs, she'd stood regal as a queen. Now, straight-backed as could be, she walked away as if she were picking her way past rotted jetsam instead of a wealth of imports. He shook his head and heaved a deep sigh. "Where do they come from?"

"That was quite some yarn she spun," Franklin said.

"The woman's probably desperate to attempt such a ploy. Lame, thin, and wan as can be, she probably can't find either a job or a husband." John took a gold piece from his pocket and absently ran his thumb across the surface. 'Twas more money than she'd likely seen in several months, but he'd not even feel its loss. She didn't deserve anything for her scam; yet she must be in dire straits to have conjured up such a plan—unless there really was a hungry babe. Christ taught compassion instead of judgment. "Go give this to her."

Later, when Franklin returned, he trundled over and shoved his hands in his pockets. "The woman gave me a message for you. She promises to pay back every last cent."

John scoffed. "That promise is about as honest as her woeful tale."

Franklin rubbed the furrows in his forehead. "I almost believed her. She clutched your coin tight in her fist and said, 'The O'Briens hold honor dear. They don't take charity.' "

John dismissed her words and set to work. Newcomb Shipping demanded his full attention. Fine Virginia cotton, wool, and hemp awaited loading into the hulls of the *Peregrine.* The *Allegiant,* now full of wheat, Indian corn, tobacco, and oats, required one last inspection ere she set sail. In a nearby berth, dockhands scurried to offload the coffee the *Gallant* imported from Rio. The stench of tar and turpentine wafted past as the wind shifted—a reminder that he needed an update on the *Osprey*'s repairs. John strode down the dock and set out his priorities for the day.

The very next morning, Franklin handed John a note. "A lad brought this for you."

Intrigued, John unfolded the smudged paper and caught a penny as it slid out.

> *Dear Mr. Newcomb,*
>   *I'll be faithful to pay you back.*
>   *O'Briens don't take charity.*

The brave little woman's words echoed in John's mind. She hadn't behaved as he'd expected her to. He'd thought she'd taken him for a soft touch, but she'd sent back this penny—a mere pittance. Was she hoping to reel him in for more?

As the day crawled on, her words kept haunting him. *Anna gave him a son. . .married. . .while he's been larking around, his wife's dinner plate was empty. . . .* What if he'd misjudged the poor girl? Maybe she hadn't been trying to make fraudulent accusations in hopes of getting money. Was it possible one of the *Cormorant*'s crewmen actually misrepresented his identity and she believed her cause to be just? The sincerity in her tone and the look in her expressive green eyes certainly rang true.

The *Cormorant* had set sail on a prolonged voyage, so John couldn't even pose questions of Edward for several months. If the woman's plight was as dire as she'd implied, she couldn't wait for assistance. John determined to gather some facts. He sent for a discreet fellow he'd used to investigate sensitive matters in the past and engaged his services.

❧

Though he normally didn't personally oversee ships' departures, two days later John stood at the dock and watched the *Resolute* leave her moorings. He'd brought down a small case of heirloom jewelry. The bequest was to reach a young woman, and he'd not wanted any chance of its disappearing, so he'd personally handed the treasures to the captain. The 4 A.M. turn of the tide made for an all-too-early awakening, but John shrugged it off. 'Twas part of his responsibility, and if ever he had a daughter, he'd want others to handle her cherished possessions with as much care.

Rather than going back home, he went into the shipping office. The register containing the contents of his warehouse lay open on his desk, but the figures of cotton bales, bushels of Indian corn, and bags of coffee beans could wait. Instead, John dragged his chair over by the stove. He'd barely started to nod off when the door opened.

"Sir, I found her—that woman you were looking for." The agent handed him a scrap of paper and slipped out the door as soon as John paid him.

Anna O'Brien, No. 6, Larkspur. Larkspur lay on the very outskirts of town, along the farthest edges of the docks—shantytown. John quickly drew on his warm greatcoat and set out. Instead of riding his horse, he took a wagon and ordered the driver to let him off about a half mile away from the address. This way he'd not have to worry his mount would be stolen. He hadn't been to shantytown since he was a callow youth. Back then it looked dreary and sordid; time only worsened its condition. A silvery half moon illuminated the frost that sparkled on everything—reminding him of an iced deck. He'd rather be on such a deck than here—'twas less chancy than wandering this district.

"Wretched" described Larkspur perfectly. The dwellings were nothing more than shanties knocked together out of salvaged scraps of wood. Bitterly cold, tangy ocean air whistled between them; and ramshackle as they looked, John marveled, as he did every time he saw them, that they didn't blow over. One stood like a polished pebble amidst the rubble. Number Six. He stared at the gray, weathered boards. Not a weed grew around them. In fact, a few flowers and tangled squash vines struggled to endure against the late autumn wind. He made a fist, then reconsidered. The wooden door was rough. No use getting splinters in his knuckles. Instead he used his boot to kick lightly on the widest plank.

two

"Just a minute," a sleepy voice bade.

Seconds passed while John impatiently flicked his gloves against his thigh. Each of his exhalations fogged on the cold, cold air. Even wrapped in the folds of his thick greatcoat, the air's icy bite penetrated to the skin. Across the way, the eyes of rats gleamed red like ingots fresh from Hades. Steps sounded, and a high-pitched voice asked, "Who is it?"

"John Newcomb."

" 'Tis John Newcomb, Anna. Do I let him in?"

Lamplight shone through small cracks in the house, so it came as no surprise that each word could be heard through the rattletrap boards. Thin wails of a babe wavered the air. Anna must have nodded because a latch slid free moments later, and a lanky boy with a sleep-tousled, red mop of hair peered out from behind a mere crack in the door.

"Thank you." John pushed his way in. As soon as he determined no danger existed inside the abode, he shut and secured the door. Slowly he looked about and took measure of the tiny, one-room shack. Shock rippled through him before he disciplined his features.

Such meager contents: a bed, two rickety chairs, a battered table, and a pathetic excuse for a stove. In the corner, behind a tattered bit of sailcloth that had been pushed back, a rumpled pallet lay directly on the sand-gritted flooring planks. He focused back on the bed and wondered how old the tiny woman in it might be. How could she, the lame woman, and this little lad— let alone a babe—possibly survive in circumstances this grave?

"John Newcomb," a faint voice said from the bed. "I didn't know Edward had a brother. How kind you are to come see your nephew!"

It took but three steps to reach the bedstead. The woman in it looked pitifully thin and weary, but even with those marks against her, John immediately recognized her similarity to the woman he'd met at the shipyard. Red hair and big green eyes attested that they were sisters, but her ashen skin testified that she'd been ill a long while. Just above the edge of a time-battered blanket, he spied a downy head.

The sickly woman smiled at John, then followed his gaze to look back down at her infant. "I've not named him yet. I hoped Edward would be here to help me decide on what his son is to be called." She painstakingly drew the covers back a tad. Her fourth finger, John noticed, bore no wedding band.

Was she fighting modesty or just too weak to do the minuscule task? He leaned forward and looked intently at the tiny, swaddled bundle. In no way did the babe resemble Edward. In point of fact, the babe didn't take after anyone John knew. He looked like a wizened old man as he screwed up his face and let out a tiny bleat.

"Oh, now," Anna crooned softly.

John tried not to show his surprise when a shred of paper drifted out of the pillow slip. Knowing poverty existed was one thing, but seeing this timid little woman eke by with a paper-stuffed pillow defied belief. She reminded him of a tiny mouse, nesting in shreds of paper.

"Duncan, come be a dear and check his nappy for me. The puir, wee man-child is likely wet and hungry again."

For being on the young side, little Duncan handled the task with fair grace. The lad's arms were bony, and the baby's limbs looked like nothing more than matchsticks. From what he saw, John knew no one in this household had benefited from a decent meal in a long while.

Since they were occupied, John made no apologies for snooping about. A strip of salt-flecked, discarded sail gathered on a bit of string served as a curtain on the narrow window, but discarded newspapers covered the pane in a vain attempt to insulate the shack. Two shelves hung on one side of the window. A sparse collection of mismatched dishes perched on one. The other held nothing more than a pair of bruised apples, two pint jars filled with dried leaves, and a small glass bottle with barely an inch of milk. John's brows knit as he searched in vain for evidence of any other food.

His wife's dinner plate was empty. The words echoed again in his mind. They'd not been a melodramatic exaggeration. If anything, they'd been an understatement. John's heart ached with pity, and he no longer wondered why the spirited woman had concocted her scheme to blame Edward for the paternity of the babe. She came to his shipyard desperately needing to feed her family—but where could she be? And why had she paid back a penny when she should have bought food with it? What else had she done with the money?

He opened the stove and stirred the embers. The coal bucket next to the stove held one last small clump—certainly not enough to keep them warm for even half an hour more. He tossed it in, did his best to fasten the tiny grated door that hung askew and asked in a deceptively casual tone, "Where is your sister?"

"She'll be home soon," Duncan answered. He tucked the baby in the bed. "There, then, our Anna. You were right about your wee little fellow wanting his supper. He's chewing on his fist. Put your arm about my shoulder. I'll help you turn a bit."

John watched the lad take his sister's frail, linen-covered arm and hook it about his own scrawny neck. Together they looked like a small heap of snowed-upon kindling. The lad didn't look half big enough to move her.

Propriety dictated John should turn his back. Anna O'Brien was a stranger, dressed in her nightgown, and lay in bed no less. A man of decency would never call upon a woman still in her childbed unless she were close family. Though circumstances rated as far less than fully proper, John couldn't stand by and allow this poor woman and her kid brother to struggle. "I'll help."

A smile brightened the lad's somber face. "Thank you, Sir."

After Duncan stepped out of the way, John learned firsthand that Anna's profound weakness kept her from raising her own arms. Even after he stooped and gently lifted her arm, she could scarcely cup her hand about his neck. When he turned her, thin shoulder blades jutted out like bird wings beneath her gown. She shivered, not from his touch, but from the drafts coming through the walls. He gingerly tucked the babe close to the bodice of her gown and hastily situated the blanket around them. She rewarded his aid with a smile that glowed with gratitude. "Oh, you made that so easy for me. I thank you."

John tried not to show his horror at her thinness, but when the babe's wail echoed the wind whining between the walls, he asked quietly, "Do you have enough milk for the baby?"

"Not yet—but we're in the first days." A faint pink washed into her cheeks. "According to the midwife, three or four days usually pass before milk flows well."

John nodded. It wasn't that he truly agreed; he knew nothing about such matters. He did so because of the desperate hope and worry mingling in the new mother's voice. She needed privacy, so he excused himself. "The morning is cold, and your stove is near empty. I'll be back in awhile with some coal."

"Oh! You'd do that for us? You're a generous man, John Newcomb."

He ordered Duncan to latch the door behind him and waited until he heard the slat slide into the warped bracket before he strode away. This neighborhood carried a hopeless mix of the poor, the drunken, and the unsavory. His hand went naturally to the reassuring knife he wore sheathed on his belt. Years on a ship taught him how to wield it for any necessary task. Down here, protection was essential—yet Duncan and Anna lived helpless as lambs among this rabble.

The gold coin he'd given should have paid for warmth and food. Desperate as their needs were, why hadn't the other O'Brien woman used it sensibly? Her foolishness kept them hungry and cold. He shook his head in disbelief. What lunacy drove her?

John wisely came here without much jangling in his pocket. Providing such temptation would invite attack. Dawn hadn't yet broken, but the dingy thoroughfare lined with a smattering of shops sluggishly stirred to life. Lamps started to light windows and illuminate expansive boasts that the small businesses failed to fulfill. Even the bakery's fragrant aroma seemed to promise far more than simple loaves and buns.

First he purchased a basket and hooked it awkwardly over his left arm. By spending most of the paltry coins he'd brought, John determinedly filled it to overflowing. He'd done his share of bartering and marketing in dozens of ports and used that experience to make sure he got fair value for his coin. Badly as that lad and the new mother needed to eat, he'd not settle until he knew their bellies would be full.

"You there." He pointed at a stoop-backed man. "I need two full scuttles of coal taken to shanty number six, Larkspur Lane, right away."

"Aye, Sir. I'll be right on yer heels!"

John arrived back at the shack and bumped the door once before young Duncan opened it. "Bless me, Anna—he came back!" He danced an excited jig as he said in astonished wonderment, "And he brought food!"

John set the basket on the table. He'd carefully set a handful of cookies atop everything else in hopes they wouldn't get broken. The lad spied them and did the inexplicable—he backed away. "Are y–you the d–d–devil?"

"Duncan!" his sister gasped.

Eyes big as saucers, Duncan whispered, "Em says, 'God sends meat; the devil brings cookies.' Anna, he brought cookies!"

John chuckled and pulled a small ham from the basket. "There, now. Meat. Does that put your mind at ease?"

Duncan still didn't look certain. He patted his sister's leg. "What are you thinking we ought to be doing?"

"All's well, Boy-o." Anna gave John a winsome smile. "Please forgive him."

"There's nothing to forgive. Duncan is trying to protect his family." A knock sounded. John opened the door and accepted the coal.

Duncan spied the fuel. "Oh, Sir! God bless you! Anna, this'll keep the baby warm all year!"

John chortled softly at the boy's innocence and enthusiasm. He didn't have the heart to deny the claim. Indeed, he'd arrange for coal to be delivered so Anna, her wee babe, and little Duncan would be warm for as long as they needed. He quickly added coal to the stove, wishing it wouldn't need time before the fire would catch and radiate more heat.

John pulled a slightly bent knife from the shelf. After the first cut, he traded it for his belt knife and sliced the loaf of bread and cheese. Ham had never been hacked into sorrier slabs, but he felt sure neither Anna nor Duncan would notice. He handed the lad some bread.

"Get water so I can put the eggs on to boil." While Duncan took a bucket and scampered outside to a communal pump, John carried the bread and cheese over to the bedside. As he gently lifted Anna's shoulders and head, he realized Duncan had taken his own blanket and spread it atop her.

Before Anna accepted a bite, she paused and dipped her head. Her pale lips moved silently in what he presumed to be a prayer. Though he knew she was half-starved, she took dainty bites from his hand. Her eyes shone with gratitude.

Duncan returned and filled a small pot, then set the eggs to boil. The remainder of the water went into a chipped porcelain pitcher. He gobbled up another slice of bread. "Soon as the eggs are done, I'll make you some tea. I'll cool the rest of the water a bit, and we can wash up the babe, too."

"You're a fine uncle, Duncan," Anna praised. She looked up at John and whispered, "As are you, John Newcomb. I've prayed for Edward to come home, but the Lord surely sent you in the meantime. You're an unexpected answer to my supplications."

John gave no reply. He'd made no claim to the babe and promised nothing; yet he felt guilty as a thief. After setting foot here, he could easily see why they sought a male connection. He never should have come. He wasn't a man to indulge in deception; yet his very presence hinted at a relationship that didn't exist.

He knew his brother well. Edward appreciated quality things, cultured women, and monied society far too much to consort with an impoverished, skinny Irish lass. Clearly, someone had hornswoggled this poor girl, but he knew it wasn't Edward's doing. Relief sifted through him that his brother wouldn't do such a contemptible thing. Despite his compassion and pity for the occupants of this shack, John refused to pretend any connection.

He finished feeding her slivers of ham, a small hunk of cheese, and the bread, then laid her back down. In his younger years, he'd seen a ship that had been caught in the Doldrums and the sailors nearly starved. They'd gorged on food and become violently ill. As a result of that memory, he hesitated to offer her more. She'd barely eaten enough for a small child; yet she seemed quite satisfied.

"Oh, I thank you. That was wondrous good."

"There's more. You need to eat tiny meals several times a day to build up your strength."

"I've had gracious plenty. We'll save the rest for Emily."

Oh, so her name is Emily.

"There's lots for Em," Duncan said as he stood on tiptoe to peer into the kettle and check on the eggs. John clasped the boy's thin frame and lifted him away. He was far too short—couldn't they see he'd likely scald himself? *But what choice do they have? Where is Emily, and why isn't she here, tending these two?*

Duncan traipsed over to the bed. "Emily could eat all day and night. The whole basket is brimming. Mr. Newcomb brought us a feast, our Anna."

Anna's thin face lit with delight. "God be praised! We'll have a bit to eat on the morrow. Mr. Newcomb, you're too kind!"

"Rest," John bade gruffly. It pained him to see a woman so starved that she thought to ration such a modest offering. He'd filled the basket with whatever could be found, but this fare rated as exceedingly plain. The total of its contents was far less than the waste from his own table each day.

Cold seeped through the walls. He felt awkward covering Anna, but she'd weakly slumped onto her back again and needed warmth in the worst way. Her linen gown looked threadbare. He'd never given any thought to the bedding in his home, but one of his blankets measured thicker than both on her bed, combined. As he tugged the blankets up higher and tucked them beneath her shoulders so they'd capture whatever meager heat she had, she shivered. From the appreciative, trusting look on her face, he knew it wasn't a shiver of apprehension, but one of pure, cold misery. "More coal," he muttered to himself. "We need to warm up this place."

He strongly considered smashing a chair and adding it to the stove. The dry wood would catch and blaze quickly until the coal finally burned well. A single glance at the furniture in the place established the fact that not a single piece was worth salvaging. He'd use one of the chairs first. From the looks of them, one solid whack, and they'd shatter.

Before he could rise and carry out that plan, the door rattled. Having knelt to tend the coals, John needed to crane his neck to see past the table. The woman from the dock limped in. Worry creased her face, and he strongly suspected the redness of her nose and eyes wasn't just from the cold. She forced a smile that didn't begin to hide the worry in her big, green eyes. "What are my two loves doing up so very early?"

"Em! He came!"

She perked up and avidly scanned the tiny shanty. "Edward? Where?"

From the bed Anna said, " 'Tisn't my Edward, but it's the next best, Emily. My Edward has a brother! His name is John, and he came."

"He brought food and coal!"

Emily bristled. She stared at the basket, then said, "O'Briens don't take charity!"

John stood. "One could scarcely call it a charity, Miss O'Brien."

Her gaze bore right through him. "Oh, so you've decided we might be family now, have you?" She pulled a scarf from her head and shook out a fire fall of breathtakingly beautiful, thick, auburn hair.

Brazen, he thought. He stared straight back and felt a wave of disgust. What other work did a woman do at night but to be a harlot? His voice took on a sharp edge. "I've decided nothing."

A sharp gasp sounded from the bed off to his side. Anna's reaction accused him of hideous cruelty, for he'd just served her a terrible—if unintentional—insult. Too weak even to care for herself, the poor girl-woman now suffered from his temper, too. He'd just slurred her character in the worst way imaginable simply because he'd tried to take the starch out of her sister. Shame flooded him.

Emily opened the door. Her glower could set a bonfire. "Please leave."

He'd go, though first he owed Anna his apology. John looked over at her, but Duncan slipped between them. His little face puckered with confusion, but he took his sister's cue and tried to protect Anna.

"Emily," the little boy said, "I don't understand."

Anna began to weep.

"He started out by being so nice." Duncan's voice carried a plaintive tone. "He's Edward's brother, and he brought us food!"

Emily cast a glance at the basket on the table, then back at John. Weariness mingled with bitterness in her tone. "Duncan, he isn't here because he thinks we're family. He intended it as charity."

"Stop this nonsense and shut the door," John snapped. The woman had no more sense than a brick to be letting what little heat they had in the shack escape. Didn't she notice every breath any of them took condensed into a fog?

She adamantly shook her head. "Not until you're on the other side."

"Now see here!"

"No, you see here," Emily said in an unrelenting tone. "Edward Newcomb married Anna. I'll not let you insult my sister or besmirch her name."

"You have proof of this marriage?"

Contrary to her earlier assertion, Emily shut the door. The whole wall shook. "Aye, we do." She hastily tied her scarf back over her remarkable hair in a belated move of modesty, limped over to the far side of the bed, and produced a small fabric bag he'd spied earlier. From it she drew out a black book. Most of the gold from the lettering had long since rubbed off. For a second she reverently passed her chapped hand on the battered-looking leather cover, then laid the Bible on the bed and opened it. "We recorded Anna's nuptials here, and—"

"I'm not about to accept that as proof." John marveled at her gumption. Did she think him so gullible that he'd stupidly accept such a poorly executed sham? "Anyone can write whatever they jolly well please!"

"Not in the Holy Scriptures," Duncan protested, his voice full of shock.

"If that isn't good enough, then the license will speak for itself!" Emily took a folded sheet of paper out and smoothed it open. "Seeing as you're hostile, I'll thank you to step away from the fire ere I hand this over."

John made an impatient noise and reached her side. Stiff and straight as she stood, she barely cleared his shoulder. John resisted the urge to swipe the paper from her. Matters in this pitiable household were already strained enough without his acting like a brute—though he rather felt like one for having upset sickly little Anna. Try as he might, he couldn't block out the muffled sounds of her weeping. Nevertheless, he had to focus on the principal matter at hand. He stared at the page Emily laid on the bed and scowled. "This is nonsense!"

"Nay, 'tis Latin." Emily's tone carried a rich tang of sarcasm. Her hand shook as it hovered over the flower-embellished parchment. She pointed at several places but didn't actually touch the document. "Here. The vicar's signature. Here. Anna's. Mine. Edward's and our neighbor Leticia's. There were witnesses, so the marriage is legal as can be."

"My brother's middle name is Timothy, not Percival." He ignored the impatient flash in her eyes that accused him of concocting a falsehood and looked back at the signatures. The application of their tutor's ruler to the back of Edward's hand taught him superb penmanship. John scowled. "Whoever signed this wasn't my brother. The scrawl on this is scarcely legible. Furthermore, if this is a marriage certificate, I'm a chamber pot. The Latin on here is a collection of words that mean nothing at all. 'Tis sheer gibberish."

The jut of Emily's chin made it clear she didn't believe him. Her hand dove back into the bag once again. Out it came. Between her calloused thumb and blistered forefinger, she held a ring. "And this? You cannot deny a family ring!"

John's breath caught. He took the ring from her. The thin band of gold held nothing more than a little ruby chip in the center. As jewelry went, the piece was cheap as could be, but John had given a similar ring to his governess when he was younger than Duncan. He recalled his mother taking him to a jeweler's, where there had been dozens of such rings with either rubies or sapphires. He'd thought the pinkish red stone fitting for a woman, so he'd chosen one of the ruby ones.

"Where did you get this?" He fought the ridiculously strong urge to curl his fingers and keep the sentimental little piece, even though there was no proof it was the one he'd once given. Undoubtedly hundreds of women owned such rings.

"It's Anna's wedding band, it is. Edward Newcomb himself

put it on her finger. He said it had belonged in his family for generations. Anna grew afraid her pretty wedding band would slip off because she'd gotten so thin, so we kept it here for safety." Emily snatched it back. She meticulously put everything back into the bag.

"You've given me no real proof, Emily. Newcomb isn't an uncommon name. I could ride just one day's direction either way and find a good half dozen Newcombs. A man with a name similar to my brother's duped your sister. That is a pity, to be sure, but those facts and your so-called evidence aren't nearly enough to convince me a true and holy marriage exists between my brother, Edward Timothy Newcomb, and Anna."

Emily's jaw hardened. "Sir, take yourself out of here."

John tore his gaze from hers. He glanced up at the pillows. Beneath the covers, Anna's much-too-thin shoulders continued to jerk with every muffled sob she took. The babe began to cry.

"Now see what you've done?" Emily whispered hotly. "Begone!"

"And take this with you!" Duncan swept the basket from the table and shoved it at him. John's hands automatically closed around the handle. The little boy hadn't let go of the basket. He put all of his puny weight behind it to force John out. The effort didn't actually work, but John saw no point in tarrying where he wasn't wanted. He no more than stepped outside, and the door slammed shut.

three

He stood outside the shack and heard Emily's voice suddenly alter pitch. It went soft and wooing, carrying a gentle comfort only devoted love could produce. "There, now, our Anna. Never you mind that man. No, don't you mind him at all. We know the truth, and God does, too. That's what matters. Why, your sweet little son is all upset about his mama crying. Here, let me help the pair of you."

The baby wailed a minute more, then fell silent. A few moments later, the cries began again. John knew essentially nothing at all regarding babes, but even a fool knew they needed milk. Unless Anna suddenly had sufficient meals, she'd never have enough to suckle her child.

Duncan's guilty voice carried through the cracks. "Our Em, we didn't know. We didn't know he was bad. No, I never would have guessed it at all. You know, we got so excited, we even ate his food."

"Well, now, you needn't confess it so shamefully, Boy-o. You didn't know. 'Twas an honest mistake you made. I'll still pray God blesses each and every morsel you swallowed. Go on ahead and take your full belly back to bed."

The boy's voice carried uncertainty. "I forgot about the eggs he gave us. I boiled them. Want me to pitch them out the door?"

"There's no use wasting good food." Emily sighed.

John quietly set the basket down by the door, but as he stepped away, he caught movement out of the corner of his eye. Rats. They'd take every last crumb. That didn't matter as much as the fact that he didn't want to lure the vermin to the shack, so he swept it back up and glowered at the closed door.

It wasn't his problem. He'd given her a gold coin and didn't expect repayment. He'd brought food and coal. That was enough. He owed them nothing.

John walked off.

He strode down past the other shanties to a busy street and hailed a passing carriage. Running his shipping business took all of his time and energy. If he didn't get moving, he'd not complete reviewing the manifests for the shipments due to go out on the next tide. Though his clerk could handle most matters and John trusted him well enough, a few transactions specifically demanded his presence or attention today.

Two hours later, John slammed the *Freedom*'s log shut. He couldn't concentrate. The basket of food in the corner nagged at him. Anna's soft weeping and Duncan's outrage haunted his conscience. Even if Emily sniped at him like a shrew, her brother and sister seemed nice enough.

He'd left in a temper, trying to convince himself they weren't his problem; but now that he'd cooled off, John felt differently. A Christian man owed the less fortunate his assistance. He'd never seen anyone more destitute than they. He decided to go back and offer little Duncan a job. Though no bigger than a minnow, the lad could carry messages and empty waste bins. That way they'd have a bit of money coming in, and the sacred O'Brien pride would be spared.

John didn't have time to go back to the shack so he sent Franklin to fetch Miss Emily. "Bring her here and don't take no for an answer. She may fuss, but in the end she'll relent." He glanced at the basket and decided it would be best not to send it along as a reminder of the disastrous visit.

"I'll go at once, Sir."

"Stop on your way to buy them more coal, a hearty meal,

and a few quarts of milk. Leave the offering on their table. If they refuse it, point out that they cannot afford this misplaced pride. Regardless of whatever qualms Miss Emily holds, Miss Anna must eat to feed her baby son."

Franklin nodded somberly. John knew he could trust him to carry out his orders to the letter. Not only that, Franklin was a man of discretion. He'd not make this trip a matter of conjecture or gossip. Satisfied he'd fulfilled his Christian duties, John opened the ship's log and once again pored over the entries.

Franklin came back later—alone. Though normally rather impassive, he folded his arms across his chest and reported in a vexed tone, "I did some mighty fancy talking to make the small boy let me in. Miss Anna's lying abed with her newborn. I did not find Miss Emily at home, and when I inquired after her, the lad said she was at work; but before I could ask where, his sister shushed him. She seemed. . .ashamed."

"I'm not surprised," John muttered darkly.

"Neither the lad nor Miss Anna would say another word as to her whereabouts. The men at the docks probably gauged her correctly when they presumed her to be a doxy."

"She has no business gallivanting around. Her sister and that babe need her help."

Franklin grimaced. "Deplorable as the place is, I can see why she'd not be eager to spend her day there. At least they'll have enough coal to stay warm."

"What about the food?"

"The lad acted a bit stubborn, but I repeated your message. Bone thin, they are. I took gracious plenty and felt like I should have taken triple. The little mother looked down at her babe and told the boy they'd have to accept the food. Hungry though she must be, she instructed him to hold back some for their sister."

"After you left their abode, did you investigate the neighborhood and interview others to determine Emily's whereabouts?"

Franklin shrugged. "They're a closed-mouthed lot down there. I asked a few folk and might as well have been speaking a different language entirely. They pretended not to understand me or know a thing."

"You did as well as I could reasonably expect," John said. "Mayhap Emily will think to contact me when she sees fit to go home."

"I gave them the message that you want her to pay a visit here."

John nodded acknowledgment and turned back to his work. The day passed, but Emily never made an appearance. Thoroughly irked by her absence and probable occupation, John went out of his way to swing by Larkspur that evening. Duncan stood with his arms and legs spread in the doorway like a landlocked squid to bar his entrance. "Em said you're not allowed to talk to our Anna." He glowered. "You made my sister cry."

John couldn't very well argue with the truth—especially one as galling as that. He compressed his lips for a moment, then nodded. He looked at the lad. Duncan was a strange mix of belligerence, innocence, and protectiveness. John leaned closer and said in a low tone, "I'm here to offer you a job. Do I speak man-to-man with you?"

"Em won't have it." The lad cast a worried look over his shoulder. "Besides, I have to stay home because Anna and the babe need my help."

John glanced at the bed. Anna's face looked white as a sail in the moonlight. He whispered a quick prayer of thanks that she continued to sleep through his visit. The last thing he wanted was to upset her again.

"Duncan, I could pay you a bit in advance now for the

labor you'd do later. I'd trust you to work it off."

The lad's scrawny fingers curled more tightly around the doorjamb. The unpainted wood had aged and dried until it looked gray as thunderclouds. "My sister wouldn't like me talking to you. No, she wouldn't. Last night you tricked me. I thought you were a good man, and I let you in our house. I won't let you fool me again. Go away." Behind him the babe let out a tiny squeal. Duncan slipped back inside and shut the door. A scraping sound let John know Duncan slipped the small bar latch into the bracket to lock him out.

John walked to the end of Larkspur, then turned back to look at the shanty. The betrayal he'd read on Duncan's face ate at him. Somehow he'd make amends. Distasteful as it might be, the truth was, he'd have to deal with Emily. John hired a runner to keep watch on the house and fetch him when she finally returned.

Word didn't come until three-thirty the next morning.

Short of sleep and shorter still of temper, John dressed quickly and set out to serve the older O'Brien sister a big slice of his mind. What business did she have, leaving an ailing sister, a newborn babe, and a small lad alone all hours of the day and night? He'd wanted a few more hours of sleep himself; but if he didn't catch her now, who knew when she'd see clear to checking back in with her kin? He reached the dilapidated shack and didn't even bother to knock.

From being inside, he knew precisely where the bracket and stick were affixed to lock the door. John took the knife from his belt, slipped it between the door and its brittle frame, lifted the latch, and kneed the rough wooden panel.

Hopefully, Anna, Duncan, and the baby would be sleeping. He'd get Emily to come outside to discuss matters with him. It might well be her brother and sister didn't know how she spent her time, and he'd get more honest information from her away from their hearing.

The door creaked open. He slipped in and shut it behind him right away. Though a large man, he'd learned to move silently long ago. Now that ability stood him in good stead.

After allowing his eyes a moment to readjust to the dark, John noted Duncan slept in a tight huddle on his floor pallet. Though definitely warmer than it had been on his first visit, the shanty remained chilly. *Why didn't I think to have Franklin bring blankets for them, too?* John heaved a silent sigh. He should have ordered Franklin to tell them he'd continue to send coal. No doubt they'd rationed it to make it last, just as they had the food.

John's gaze fell upon the food shelf, and the contents of his warehouses scrolled through his mind. Flour, oats, corn, salt, coffee, molasses, syrup, and sweet potatoes he had aplenty. He'd convince Emily to send Duncan to work at the shipyard, and each payday John would contrive for a supply of those staples to be part of the lad's earnings. That arrangement ought to salvage the O'Brien pride.

John continued to scan the room. The small lump in the bed had to be Anna. Where was Emily? Had she gone out again?

Disgusted, John decided at least to add a bit of coal to the stove so the fire wouldn't burn out and force them to awaken to a cold home. He took care to move silently in order to keep from awakening Duncan or the baby. As for Anna—well, he seriously doubted she'd stir at all. After John rounded the table, he stopped dead in his tracks.

Emily sat on the floor with her back to the wall. Her head rested against the side of the bed, her magnificent hair billowing in loose, coppery waves to her hips. Thick auburn lashes lay in crescents on her cheeks, and her lips bowed upward in a charming half-smile, making him wonder where her dreams carried her. A bitsy, half-made, white garment rested in her lap. The threaded needle still dangled from the minuscule sleeve, glinting in the dull light of the stove. She'd fallen asleep while trying to do something more for her tiny nephew. That loving task tugged at John's heart.

The dockhands and Franklin all thought she was a harlot, and her nighttime absence from the shanty confirmed that deduction. As much pride as Emily O'Brien displayed, it probably wounded her something fierce to sell herself; but her love for her siblings undoubtedly drove her to a woman's most unsavory profession. Faced with no other choice, she'd sacrificed herself for them. What else could she have done? Without a father or older brother to provide for them, Emily had to bring in money. No one would have hired her as a maid or laundress since she was lame and had the rest of her family to tag along.

In the still of the night, standing over her, John decided he'd lift the burden of providing for them from her shoulders so she could revert to a decent manner of living. He'd give her that chance. 'Twas a sound plan. Christ gave the woman at the well an opportunity to change her life. John would follow the Savior's example. If he approached this situation with mercy and compassion, she could listen to the gospel and turn her life back around.

Emily moaned ever so softly in her sleep, and as she shifted, the hem of her ugly brown dress caught on something. Her breath hitched, and she moved her limb a bit. A soggy cloth plopped from her ankle onto the floor.

John choked back a bellow. From the soft glow of the stove, he could see her foot and ankle were blackish-violet and hideously swollen. Though he wasn't a man to gawk at a woman's limbs, her calf looked far too thin—even before he compared it to her bloated ankle. How could she bear to walk on that?

He leaned forward and looked more closely. 'Twas a very recent injury. His mouth went dry. *She fell at the shipyard.* He winced because he couldn't even recall asking if she'd harmed herself. *All this time I assumed she'd been lame for years; but 'tis a new injury, one that requires pampering so it can heal. How does she bear to walk on it at all?*

Just as he began to kneel at her side, she startled awake. A terrified shriek erupted from her, and she tried to strike him.

four

"Emily! Stop. Stop!" He captured her wrists and gave her a moment to discover his identity and gather her wits; then he slowly released his hold. "I didn't mean to alarm you."

"Emily?" Anna whispered in a quavering tone.

"Want me to bop him?" Duncan stood just out of reach and gripped a pan in both hands.

"There's no need for that, Lad," John said. For all of his intentions to sneak in and hold a whispered conversation, he'd managed to rouse everyone in the home—well, nearly everyone. Though he'd even startled Anna awake, the babe managed to sleep on.

John watched Emily struggle to quell the residual panic. Eyes huge, she stared at him and swallowed hard. Her narrow shoulders heaved with her rapid, deep breaths. Had he awakened with someone hovering over him, he knew he'd have swung to protect himself. Striving to inject a soothing tone to his voice, he reassured her, "Truly you've no need to be afraid."

Duncan scampered around to Emily's other side and clutched the pan to his scrawny chest. He didn't seem to be in any hurry to relax his guard. "My Em isn't ever scared. She's brave and strong, she is!"

Brave? Yes, he'd agree with that, but unafraid and strong—she was neither of those. Even so, John found Duncan's faith in his big sister endearing. Whatever her flaws might be, Emily had certainly earned the loyalty and love of her little brother.

Emily. John focused on her and fought the temptation to

smooth back a springy wisp of hair that fell forward on her much-too-pale cheek. Instead he straightened up, clasped his hands behind his back, and kept his gaze on poor Emily. "All is well, Duncan. I just came to talk to your sister."

"No, I'll not let you speak to her—not now, not ever." Emily looked up at him and resolutely shook her head. "You already said more than enough the last time you came here."

"I wanted to speak to you," John clarified, "not Anna."

Anna looked up at him. Her eyes glistened with tears. "Emily is tired. Go away."

"I won't take much of her time."

"She has only three hours to sleep before she goes back to work," Anna whispered. "Leave her be. Leave us all alone."

John looked back at Emily. "Where do you work?"

"Wilken's—"

"Silence, Duncan!" Emily ordered.

John's jaw dropped. "The asylum? You work with those raving lunatics?" Wilken's Asylum sprawled across a fenced-in lot just down the street.

Emily's jaw jutted forward. " 'Tis no fault of their own that their minds snapped. You can think of them as wretched or miserable, but they are God's children just as much as you and I are."

"They're not safe!"

"So in your opinion they are undeserving of sound meals, a kind word, or a clean place to live? Christ said, 'Whatever ye do for the least of these brethren, you have done unto me.' "

He rocked back on his heels. She had a point, but he didn't cotton to the notion of such a young, vulnerable woman working in that kind of place. Those people could be violent! "What do you do there?"

"Honest work, 'tis, but hard," Anna whispered from the bed. "Cooking and cleaning. Soon as I get back on my feet,

I'll go back and start cooking again. Em will watch the baby for me during the day; then she'll only have to work at night to do the cleaning."

John jolted at the underlying implication. "Emily, you can't mean to tell me you cook for all of those unfortunates and clean that whole place by yourself."

"Shush!" Emily cast a quick glance at the bed.

"With your limb like that?!"

"Mr. Newcomb! Have you no decency?"

"Emily?" The paper-stuffed pillow rustled as Anna turned to her sister. "What does he mean?"

Emily picked up the baby gown, thrust the needle through the hem, and set it aside. Thoroughly irritated, she lifted the sodden cloth and glowered at him. He took her meaning and turned his back. He heard the small gasp she muffled and knew binding her ankle had to hurt—but she couldn't possibly walk on it without the support of the bandage. Next came a rhythmic, whispering *swish, swish, swish.* The cadence matched the tick of his pocket watch. Though he couldn't identify the sound, John figured he owed her a few moments of privacy.

The moment he heard her start to rise, he turned about and assisted her to her feet; but once she was upright, he surprised Emily by bracing her against his side.

"Mr. Newcomb!" She tried to pull away.

John tightened his hold, cinched her to himself, and murmured, "You need help balancing. Stop sounding so scandalized. I declare, you're half frozen!"

She gritted her teeth and said in an icy undertone, "Is there anything else you'd like to be saying to upset my youngers?"

The moment the words were out of his mouth, he regretted them. Obviously Emily hid whatever harsh realities she could from her siblings. Not that she could shield them from much.

There were no more blankets in this poverty-stricken shack. Emily made sure her siblings stayed as warm as possible, even though it meant she'd suffered.

He looked at her, and she stared straight back at him. Vexation danced in her vivid green eyes. So did wounded pride. Those things registered, but so did something else: Emily O'Brien was nothing more than skin and bones. Her full skirt, billowing apron, and shawl might well hide the full extent of the truth; but as he held her close, she couldn't disguise the fact that she was—quite literally—starving.

"Duncan," he addressed the boy in a clipped, no-nonsense tone, "I'm taking your sister outside to the oak stump. We're going to have a private talk. You're to bring out Anna's shawl to help keep her warmer. After you do, I want you to add more coal to the stove and heat up some milk for Emily."

"The milk is for Anna and Duncan. They need it; I don't."

John scowled at Emily. He understood she didn't want her brother and sister to realize how dire matters were. They'd already thought to save food for her, but John seriously doubted they had any notion how frail their stalwart sister was. He'd been fooled, and he possessed a sharp eye; love and Emily's acting ability, no doubt, blinded her siblings. He'd keep this secret for now, but he wanted Emily to know he wasn't going to back down. "We'll discuss this outside."

Weakly, Anna tried to prop herself up on one arm. "You don't have to go talk to him if you don't want to, Em."

"Yes, she does." He gave no chance for dissent. John kept hold and shepherded Emily toward the door. As long as she cooperated and hobbled alongside him, he'd let her walk; but if she dared balk, he'd sweep her into his arms. The temptation to do so was strong; yet he tamed it so she could keep her siblings in the dark awhile longer about her own sad condition. John guided her straight out of the hovel and over to a log. He set her carefully to the side, fully intending to take the place next to her.

Duncan trotted in his wake. John accepted the shawl, wrapped it about Emily, then jerked his head toward the shack in a silent order for him to leave. The little lad didn't cow easily. He braced his feet a bit farther apart and looked to his sister.

"I'm fine enough, Duncan. Go on now. Help Anna with the babe. The wee fellow ought to be waking soon." The moment Duncan shut the door, John sat to Emily's windward side and pulled her close once again. Hopefully, he'd give her a bit of shelter and some of his warmth.

She wiggled. "Turn loose of me. I've no business sitting by your side."

"Save your breath for something that matters." John kept his arm about her and reached across with his free hand to tug her sister's shawl up a little to protect her throat. He marveled at the blush the moon illuminated on her cheeks. For all of her boldness, she actually possessed a shy streak!

The swishing sound he'd heard when he turned his back suddenly made sense. A braid nearly thick as his wrist now trailed over her shoulder, and a scarf covered her head. She'd taken that moment of privacy to tame her fiery hair properly and cover it. He'd spent the last two days thinking this modest little bit of goods was a doxy? The contrast between his wild imaginings and the mild truth forced him to realize he'd misjudged her badly.

Her stomach growled.

"When was the last time you ate?"

She didn't meet his eyes. "I couldn't say. I don't own a timepiece."

"Then how is it Anna knows you're to be back at work in three hours?"

"Mr. Shaunessey next door has a mantel clock. We can hear

the chimes." She lifted her chin. "You'll find we don't lie, Mr. Newcomb, so you may as well leave off on trying to pounce on each matter as if you can capture us in something dishonest."

Her pluck won his grudging respect. This woman had mettle and fire. Still, he couldn't afford to smile and let her get away with this travesty. It was past time someone stopped her from trying to bilk blameless sailors, and it seemed circumstances had played out so he'd be the man who did precisely that. She wiggled ever so slightly, and the frailty of her build struck him anew. "You're so skinny you'd slip right through a fishing net."

"Waking me just to serve insults is hardly gentlemanly."

He muttered under his breath.

"Your opinion is not gentlemanly, either." She tried to push away.

John held her fast. "My apologies, Miss O'Brien. I came to settle some matters, but you have a penchant for disappearing. The ridiculous hours you keep make it impossible for me to connect with you at a decent time."

"Moaning about it doesn't change things, John Newcomb. Now that you've gotten my ear, could you please be hurrying with whatever it is you need to say?"

"I want to hire Duncan."

Shivers rattled her against his side. John wasn't sure whether fear or cold caused them. He wrapped his other arm about her, hoping to share his warmth with her. In bringing her out here, away from her brother and sister's hearing, he'd inadvertently opened her up to scrutiny if anyone happened to see them together. John regretfully ceased holding her in both arms and quickly dismissed the idea of opening his coat to share it with her. That would be just as ruinous.

"Nay."

Emily's words jarred his attention back to the matters on hand. "Nay?"

"I pledged to pay you back. Duncan's not going to work off my debt."

"You're not indebted to me, Emily. The coin was—"

"Charity," she clipped off.

"A gift," he corrected in a coaxing tone. "And I'll be offended if you give back another cent. We both know you didn't spend it on yourself. Tell me why you didn't use that last penny to buy food."

"Your coin took care of our rent and the midwife's fee. As for food—we had enough to get by until I'm paid tomorrow."

"If Duncan works for me, you'll not have to suffer any hungry days."

She shook her head. "I won't put Duncan out to work. He's too young yet. Besides, Anna needs his help for herself and the babe while I'm gone. She cannot even get out of bed."

"How old is he?"

"Not quite seven years."

"As long as I'm being ungentlemanly, I'll ask: How old are you and your sister?"

"You're right." She stiffened. "That is ungentlemanly."

"You scarcely strike me as the coy type."

"No, according to your estimation, I'm more the scheming-and-lying type." She paused a second, then let out a beleaguered sigh. "You're wrong, but I won't waste my time arguing with you. Your curiosity is costing me my sleep, but 'tis plain to see I'll not get one wink more 'til you get your answers. So here you are: Anna just turned seventeen, and I'm coming up on nineteen."

"Babes, the whole lot of you." His hold on her altered. He cradled her more tenderly. He'd thought Anna might have been nineteen, but Emily—he'd imagined her a good eight years older. For all of her courage, she was far too young to shoulder the burdens she carried.

John recalled having lost his parents when he was about her age. He'd been fortunate enough to have Grandfather there still to give him both a solid home and teach him the business. He hadn't been forced to scramble for each meal or worry about providing for Edward.

Emily tried to hide her yawn from him. From the looks of her, she could stand to sleep the clock around one full time, if not twice. Feeling pity for her, he asked softly, "What are you doing, living on your own?"

"Master Reilly found it cheaper to send many of us off rather than keep us. Food being scarce and no more in sight, he made his choices and stuck us on a ship."

"He couldn't separate parents and children!"

"And why not? He needed the men to till his soil. We'd been sore hungry, and Da borrowed money for food. Master Reilly called in the debt and kept my parents instead of paying for their passage. Two years we've been here."

"Had you no family along?"

Her eyes closed in grief. "On the ship my sister Maureen died of the measles."

"Poor lass," he murmured. "I'm sorry for your loss."

"Thank you." She paused a moment, drew in a deep breath, then tilted her face up to his. " 'Twas soon after we arrived, and Mr. Wilkens was kind to give Anna and me our jobs. Say what you will, but that good turn kept us going."

"He took advantage of your situation, Emily. He knew you were desperate, so he's overworked you."

"It was better than my only other choice." She looked away. "No one else would help. I took the only way available to help my family."

"So, speaking of help, who gave you the ring?" he asked even more softly.

Emily turned toward him and glared. "Your brother put it on

Anna's finger. I can see you don't believe me, and that's that." She pushed so hard, she tumbled from the log. Heated by her temper, she scrambled upright and slapped away the hand he offered to assist her. "It's a cruel man you are, John Newcomb. You find pleasure in insulting an ailing new mother, want to press a wee lad into labor, and drag a woman from her sleep just so you can dredge up her sadness until you can make her vulnerable. You've done your worst, but I'll take no more."

"Emily—"

"Back at the dock, you were willing to use your power to assure Anna's husband did right by her; but once you found out that man was your own brother, your resolve blew off like a scarf in a gale. You're a hypocrite, John Newcomb."

She held both shawls about her like a shield. "We may be poor and hungry, but we've never once stooped to dishonesty or hurt another soul. You look at us and see poverty—but you are the poorest man I ever met because your heart is empty. Don't come back here. You and your brother have done all the harm two men could e'er do."

She limped past him, and John stood aside. Her dignity and temper were a sight to behold. Two more hobbling steps, and she stumbled. He caught her arm and braced her before she hit the ground, but she didn't quite manage to stifle a whimper.

"Emily—"

With dignity worthy of a queen, she drew away and squared her shoulders. "Miss O'Brien to you." Pain drew her features taut, and tears glistened in her eyes; but she refused to let them fall. She took another step toward the house, then faltered.

He scooped her up and carried her back inside. "Until Edward returns, I'm assuming responsibility." He kicked the door shut and scowled at her. "God have mercy on your soul if I find this is all an elaborate contrivance."

five

Emily couldn't find a speck of fault with how he treated Anna. After Emily and Duncan packed everything, John Newcomb placed the bundles in a shiny conveyance he'd summoned. He came back in and spoke softly to Anna, then went back outside and waited patiently for Emily to tend to any private care her sister might need. When she sent Duncan to fetch him, John returned, gave Anna a tender smile, and promised, "Soon you'll be warm and comfortable." With surprising gentleness, he gathered the bedding and wrapped it about Anna.

He's being so good to her, Emily mused. *In all the times Edward came here, for all his smooth ways, he never seemed so genuinely caring and tender. 'Tis a crying shame 'twasn't John Newcomb who wed her. He'd make any woman a fine husband.*

John lifted Anna and carried her out to the carriage.

"Our Em, don't forget the jar," Anna whispered.

"Jar?"

Anna smiled up at him. "You're family. You can know. We've saved a wee bit to help bring Da and Mama over on the ship. Em keeps it in a jar under a floorboard."

Emily felt the accusation in his dark eyes. She turned away, and just as Duncan started to open his mouth, she pressed a finger to her lips. Duncan obeyed her silent command. She sighed with relief. She'd succeeded in silencing her brother before he'd told Anna the jar no longer held a single cent.

Even so, Emily couldn't face John. She murmured, "We've not left a thing behind," then crawled into the luxurious state carriage.

John simply gave the driver a few words of instruction and got into the conveyance. He did so with great care so neither Anna's head nor feet were bumped in the least. He slipped onto the wide, padded leather seat opposite Emily and Duncan and arranged Anna on his lap. Clearly she was too weak to sit up. He thrust a lush fur robe at Duncan. "Spread that across your laps." John then took another and gently tucked it about Anna. Her head lolled onto his shoulder, and she offered an embarrassed apology.

"Shh." The sibilant sound seemed strange coming from him. He didn't seem the type to give succor or compassion. Yet there he sat, plain as day, cradling Anna almost exactly like the stained glass window over at the church that showed Christ holding a child. Aye, and there was the reality—he might well have made a wondrous husband, but that wasn't the flavor of his actions in the least. He treated Anna with the gentle affection an uncle might bestow upon a favorite niece. Emily looked at him and hoped he'd see the gratitude in her eyes.

Their gazes caught and held. Suddenly feeling as if he were trying to see straight into her soul, she looked down at her tiny nephew and cradled him still closer to her bosom. Her hand shook a bit as she carefully tamed his fine, downy brown hair into a less wild arrangement. At her feet lay all she and her siblings owned. Against Mr. Newcomb's voluble protests, she'd taken their meager possessions and knotted them in Anna's emptied pillow slip and Duncan's blanket.

Her brother sat beside her and clutched the precious bag holding the Bible and Anna's ring. Wide-eyed, he stared out the window at the sights passing by him so quickly and crowed his interest as the city came to life for the day.

John Newcomb chuckled at something Duncan said. Emily gave him a wobbly smile, then cast a worried look out the window. "Soon as I get them settled, I'll need you to give me directions. I've gotten turned about a bit."

"Directions?"

"To the asylum."

"We'll discuss it later."

Dread snaked through her. Emily opened her mouth, then closed it as she sought the right words. After a moment's consideration, she said, "Those people are counting on me, and so is my family."

"Wilkens can find some other slave to do his bidding."

"Mr. Newcomb, the patients there need to eat!"

He made a sound of unadulterated disgust. "So did you. That miser earns a hefty sum each month to warehouse all of those unfortunates—the least he could do is hire sufficient staff and pay them decently."

"Oh, Em got a whole dollar a week!"

John's eyes narrowed at Duncan's disclosure. "Emily, you're not setting foot in that place again. I dispatched a message to him, and he knows you'll not be returning."

She moaned. "Oh, how could you do that?"

"I have four maids, and my home is a quarter of the size of that sprawling madhouse. The newest of my maids earns three times what you were paid to do that whole place on your own—and they have decent meals and warm quarters within the house."

Emily flinched at his words. She hadn't been properly trained to be a housemaid. When she'd come over on the boat, she didn't even own leather shoes. The pair she now wore were castoffs from a lunatic. Indeed, every last stitch she and her sister possessed were left by patients who died or went elsewhere.

The carriage went over a bump, and the pots rattled. She screwed up her courage. "As for cooking—"

"I'll be sure food is sent to you."

"Mr. Newcomb—" Emily tried to modulate her voice— "we cannot rely on your kindness. I'm wanting to ask if your own kitchen might be needing—"

"No."

"Laundry—"

"No," he snapped.

"I see." *He doesn't want Irish beggars working for him.* "I do hope there's some way I can—"

"You can stop formulating a stratagem this very minute." He looked meaningfully at the way Anna lay limply in his arms, then locked gazes with Emily again. "Your sister needs you. Until such time as she and the babe are hale, you're not to leave her side."

"Sir, I can take care of my sister," Duncan declared.

"Aye, and so I can see you've done your very best." His features altered into a kindly visage, and his voice slid into a man-to-man, confiding tone. "But I have a whole pack of dogs that need caring for and a favorite mare that needs special currying. You'll be busy enough already."

"A horse?" Awe filled Duncan's voice.

"A fine bay. She's particular, so you'll need to handle her well."

A lump of emotion knotted in Emily's throat. If nothing else, this would finally allow Duncan to have time to roam and play a wee bit. At best he might actually prove his value and be taken on as a stable boy. It would give him a trade—an honorable one. Da would be pleased to hear his son had such an arrangement.

Emily's eyes felt grainy, and her head weighed too heavily on her neck. She fought against leaning into the corner of the carriage and dozing. It wouldn't be proper. Besides, she needed to keep an eye on John Newcomb. He'd stepped in and started making all sorts of decisions, but she wasn't sure if she approved of them yet. Things were changing so quickly, it made her dizzy. Just when she pulled herself back from the precipice of sleep for the third time, the carriage turned off the main road, between two massive hedges, and onto a long, tree-lined drive.

A small, vine-covered cottage rested off to the north corner of the property. Nestled in a neatly trimmed, chest-high box of hedges, the clapboard's two brick chimneys thrust skyward, as if to bear testimony to John Newcomb's promise of warmth. The carriage drew up to the east side of the wondrous home and stopped.

"You ladies stay here a moment. Duncan, come with me." John gently slipped Anna onto the seat, made sure the robe kept her snug, and stepped over Emily's feet with catlike grace. He ordered the driver to hobble the horses and come back for the rig later; then he disappeared into the charming home with Duncan on his heels.

Though his caretaker's place was small, John suspected the simple cottage would seem like heaven compared to where they'd been living. It hadn't been inhabited for at least a year, and he couldn't vouch for what condition it might be in. Sheets covered the furniture, looking like ghost ships in the sea of dust.

Footprints disturbed the thick, gray coating on the floor and led to a closed door. They gave him pause to wonder who had been here. John frowned and made a mental note to instruct his staff to keep a weather eye on the place. Lovers could seek some other trysting place, for he'd not provide a place for immorality. This was to be a warm haven of rest for Emily's poor little family. The storms of life had battered them enough.

He followed the footsteps, paced to the door, and threw it wide open. No one occupied the chamber now, but it certainly had been used quite recently. Fresh, fluffy blankets covered the bed, and in contrast to the other room, no accumulated grime coated the surfaces of anything. Clearly the secret bower hadn't been just a spur-of-the-moment whim. That fact ired him even more.

"Dear me," Duncan whispered. He still stood by the front door. His rapture jarred John from his anger and caused him to see the cottage in a positive light again.

Because Anna was so infirm, the bedchamber's status rated as the most important consideration. John perused it. The bed was fair sized—certainly large enough for the sisters to share. Though the blankets on it looked fresh and heavy enough to provide sufficient warmth, he'd send over a few more so Duncan could sleep snugly as well. John nodded his satisfaction.

Duncan peered around him, marveling. "Ohh, 'tis wondrous! Does the queen live here?"

"Nay, Lad. Your sisters will."

He took Duncan's shoulder and led him a few paces toward the kitchen. A tiny alcove off to the side would serve nicely for him. "See this? You clean it up, and we'll put in a cot for you. It'll be your very own space."

The weak autumn sun barely made it past the murky windows. What little did shine through carried a host of silvery dust motes. A small shaft of light fell across Duncan's cheek as he looked up with absolute adoration. "Ooh, Sir! Your brother told us he'd get us a fine home, but I never dreamed 'twould be so verra grand!"

"Anna and her babe deserve a nice place."

"Em, too," Duncan said all too quickly. "She works so hard for us."

"Yes, especially Emily," John promptly agreed. He couldn't fault the lad for his loyalty. Since Duncan mentioned his oldest sister, John snatched the opportunity and sought more information. "Speaking of Emily, she wouldn't let you say a word about the jar. You can tell me about it, now that Anna cannot hear."

The sparkle left little Duncan's eyes. His mouth curved downward, and his voice took on a melancholy flavor. "She kept money in a jar under a loose floorboard. She spent it all. Every last cent is gone now. She tried to be ever so careful, our Em did, to save a wee bit whenever she could. But when there wasn't any more food and every last treasure got pawned, Em used part of the money to buy us food."

"What did she do with the other part?"

"Mr. Rickers wanted money for our house again. Then the midwife wanted to be paid for helping our Anna birth the babe. We didn't have enough."

John shook his head in disbelief. "You managed to save money?" The thought baffled him. In the midst of their appalling poverty, they might have just as soon hoped to fly as to try conserving money for two transatlantic passages. The notion that Emily tried to set aside even a penny wrenched his heart every bit as much as it stretched his imagination. *Yet she sent a penny back to me.*

"Aye, and we had almost half the jar filled." Duncan blinked away threatening tears. "We'd been saving hard as we could to send for Da and Mama, but Em said we'll not be able to do that for a long while now."

John nodded somberly. At least he'd gotten the truth. Yet again Emily wanted to protect her sister from the realities of their plight. He squeezed the boy's shoulder. "I think Emily wanted to keep that a secret from Anna. Are you good at keeping secrets?"

Duncan's head bobbed up and down. "I keep lots of secrets for Em."

John tugged out a small wooden chair, lifted Duncan to stand on it, and looked eye-to-eye with the lad. He dropped his tone. "Duncan, we're friends. Friends don't keep secrets. I think you'd better tell me if there's anything important I should know."

Duncan wrinkled his nose, then pursed his lips. "You won't tell Anna?"

"Never."

six

The boy leaned closer and whispered loudly, "Em pretends she's not cold, and she pretends she's full, too. It's a game, she said—but I'm not to tell Anna. I'm not supposed to tell Anna that Em cries sometimes, either. It might upset our Anna, and Em says since I'm the man in the family, it's important for me to make Anna feel happy and safe."

John nodded.

Duncan winced. "I should have asked Em first if I could tell you her secrets."

John cupped his hand around Duncan's thin shoulder. "Sharing that with me didn't break Emily's confidence in you, Duncan. She wanted to keep that a secret from Anna. I need to know things so I can help your sisters. You want that, don't you?"

The boy nodded somberly. "Em and Anna used to try to keep things from me, but that changed. Now Em and I keep things from Anna—'specially about the money. Em doesn't want Anna to know she spent it all—because now Da and Mama won't be coming for ever so long."

John schooled his features so they wouldn't betray the emotions churning through him. He looked at the lad and saw a longing in his eyes when he mentioned his mother and father. He injected a tone of cheer to his voice. "Well, Duncan-boy, 'tis true you don't have your parents with you right now; but you've been blessed to have two big sisters. And, come to think of it, standing here all day won't accomplish a thing. We'd best get them out of the carriage."

Duncan perked up. "I'll go turn back the bed!"

"You do that." John smiled as the boy brightened up, hopped off the chair, and raced toward the bedchamber. "Fold back both sides of the bed, Duncan," he called. "Emily is tired, and I want her to sleep the day away, too."

"Aye, Sir."

John reached the carriage and looked through the window. He felt a surge of anger at whomever the man was who had conned these women. Of course he expected Anna to be weary—she'd not yet recovered from her childbed, but the sight of Emily set his teeth on edge.

She'd fallen asleep, and the deep, dark circles beneath her eyes tattled at how profound her exhaustion had become. Either cooking or cleaning for that entire asylum rated as a herculean job; yet she'd done both—without decent nourishment or sufficient sleep. Awakening her was beyond cruel. He'd simply carry her in, just as he planned to do with Anna. Even in her sleep, Emily managed to cradle the babe to herself with a fierce tenderness. It wrenched his heart to think of what she'd endured to care for her little family.

Compassion still wouldn't hold back the frustration he felt. How could he have imagined a single coin would make a difference? The fact that Emily had scrimped to save a pitifully insufficient jar of coins to pay passage underscored how deeply she longed for her father to come and resume the mantle of provider and protector—the very mantle she wore of necessity. No wonder Anna wed some dashing sailor—this little family was desperate for security and provision.

The moment the well-oiled carriage door whispered open, Emily startled awake once again and banged the back of her head against the wall. "Oh, Mr. Newcomb!"

"You're exhausted. How could you possibly think you were going to work again today?"

"I'm strong."

"And I'm a mackerel," he snapped back. She started to rise, but he stopped her by lightly squeezing her bony elbow. "You dare not step down. The minute you put your weight on that mangled limb, you'll fall."

She clutched the babe to her bosom and stared at him with wide eyes. "Please take Anna first. She's fallen asleep again."

He glanced over at Anna, then turned his attention back to Emily. His eyes narrowed as he pinched the baby's blanket between his fingers and rubbed it. It had been doubled over and stitched, and he knew there were two more just like it. One draped Anna, and the other held that pathetic bundle on the floor. "Your own blanket—you cut it up for the baby."

She quickly tested the babe's skin. "Do you think he's warm enough?"

Did she ever think of herself first? John hastened to assure her that her sacrifice had been sufficient. "He's cozy as can be."

Just then the baby sneezed.

John frowned. "Let's get him inside, though. The fur will keep Anna snug for a few more minutes."

For the baby's sake, she relented. John tucked Anna's blanket and fur about her and assured himself she was far too weak to turn and fall; then he scooped Emily into his arms and drew her out. "Thank you, Sir." She fidgeted as if she expected him to set her feet down on the ground.

"Mercy!" he said in an exasperated tone as he paced to the house. "Stop trying to conquer the world. You're lame, weary, and hungry. You're to do nothing more than rest and help your sister with the baby." He took her inside and paused for a moment to let her get her bearings.

Suddenly the festooning cobwebs, inch-thick dust, and shrouded furniture looked tawdry. He'd been a fool not to have a crew of maids come over to turn the place inside out, then gone back this evening to fetch the O'Briens. Wretched as their shanty had been, they'd kept it clean. This place would send most seasoned housekeepers into a fit of the vapors. Chagrin colored his voice as he muttered apologetically, "No one has been in residence here for awhile."

"Ohh!" Emily drew out the exclamation in an expression of awe. She turned her head this way, then that, and peered over his shoulder. A deep sigh came out of her. "Mr. Newcomb, 'tis such a fine place!"

He looked at her, wondering if she was being facetious. It didn't seem so, but then he pondered whether she plastered on a smile to be polite. He couldn't mistake the truth. Emily's reaction was as guileless as it was gleeful. The way her eyes lit with undiluted pleasure delighted him no end. He no longer regretted bringing her straight here. Had he left her, she would have gone off to work and undoubtedly swooned from a combination of exhaustion, hunger, and pain. Since the dreary appearance and accumulated grime didn't bother her, he could pretend to turn a blind eye to it. He'd let her sleep, then send help on the morrow.

As he held her, he remembered her spotlessly clean shanty. He had no doubt she'd probably scrubbed that sprawling madhouse until it gleamed, too. Her hair glimmered in the sunlight, and she smelled of fresh soap and water. Oddly enough, for all the expensive perfumes women wore, he far preferred the simplicity of a woman without those cloying scents.

What in the world am I thinking, finding anything favorable about this woman? Not only did the thought jolt him mentally, he unintentionally jarred Emily.

"I'm sorry." A fetching pink suffused her cheeks. "I'm gawking around, and you need to go get our Anna."

John stepped into the bedchamber. "You'll share this room with Anna. That way you can help her at night." He took

Emily to the bed and carefully lowered her, mindful not to bump her sore ankle.

She bit her lip.

"Did I hurt you?"

Her arms anchored the babe closer still, and she stared at him for a long moment. Finally she whispered tightly, "I didn't realize the place was more than that one room. I thought maybe the cottage was cut into halves or thirds and we were to share it with other families—after all, I spied two chimneys. This is all too much. Please understand, Mr. Newcomb—I cannot afford such fine lodgings. You were so good to want better for us, but I'm sorry. This is way above my pocket."

He scowled at her. "You're not paying for this."

Her cheeks went scarlet as she choked out, "Mr. Newcomb, I'm a good woman."

A good woman. Yes, once he'd learned of her working at the asylum, he'd accepted the truth. No evidence existed of her having earned money by plying a loose woman's trade; but plenty indicated she'd twisted herself in knots, trying to care for her little family. He had assumed wrongly, and now he wondered how he could have believed such a wild notion. All of it boiled down to this awkward moment, and she felt it necessary to profess her moral standards.

Big, sincere eyes stared at him, and her face looked earnest enough. Then, too, her clothing rated as ragged, but proper and modest. She possessed nothing of value whatsoever. No two ways about it—he'd misjudged her. Now he hoped she hadn't discerned what he'd so foolishly presumed. The last thing she needed was to bear the injury of such a grievous and false accusation.

Emily started to scoot toward the far side of the bed. "I think you'd better take us back to our own house, Sir."

"No." He hastily set a hand on her arm, then reached across

and flipped the quilts to trap her on the bed. "I thought I'd been clear about the arrangements, Miss O'Brien. Until Edward returns, you, Anna, Duncan, and the babe are my guests. I'll hear no more of that. I'll go fetch Anna now."

"I thank you ever so much, Mr. Newcomb. Truly I do."

He turned to go, then hesitated. He stared at the far wall instead of facing her. "Before I fetch Anna, I must ask indelicate questions." He paused a moment to allow Emily to prepare herself for the shockingly personal things he needed to ask. No gentleman broached improper subjects with a woman, but he had no one to act as his intermediary. He whispered a quick prayer for tact. After clearing his throat, he forged ahead. "Anna's young and small, seemingly too small to birth a babe—though she obviously has. Duncan made mention of a midwife, but there are quacks aplenty who do far more damage than good. Did you summon competent help for her?"

"Aye. How could I not?"

"Good." He turned, looked down at Emily, and shrugged. "I'm not pleased with how weak she is."

"It's only been a few days, and she did have a hard time." She glanced up at him, her face etched with worry. "She's not gotten childbed fever. That's a good sign, to be sure."

He pushed ahead, although he knew the subject he broached—though necessary—was highly improper. So far Emily had been good enough not to fly into a dither over his prying. He ardently hoped she understood he asked these things only because he shared her concerns. "Has Anna's— well, is she capable—?" He drew a quick breath and blurted, "Does she have sufficient milk yet?"

"Today. It will come in today. I went to the vicar, and he got fenugreek seeds from the Benedictines for me. The tea will work."

Her face nearly glowed with embarrassment, but she actually

continued to participate in this outlandish conversation. Clearly her love for her sister and nephew overshadowed her personal discomfort. That being the case, he was going to set out his expectations.

"I put little store in most curatives, but the Benedictine monks are reputed to be gifted healers. Still, I'll not have the babe fuss for wont of milk. I'll summon an apothecary or physician to come see Anna, and you are to follow his orders precisely. If she does not have milk by the morrow, we'll engage a wet nurse."

Having spoken his piece, John left. Once outside, he breathed a prayer of thanksgiving that they'd made it over that awkward hurdle. He tugged at his collar and smiled grimly at the memory of Emily turning a rather fetching pink. Hopefully, they'd not have to discuss such delicate matters again. He wasn't sure who was more uncomfortable—but they'd made it through, and that was what counted.

John paused a moment. He looked over the lawn and past it up the drive. Set on a gentle swell of land, his mansion overlooked the ocean. It was far enough away to afford both households privacy, and he felt a spurt of relief that his home wasn't visible from this spot. The vast disparity between his wealth and the O'Briens' abject poverty couldn't be any greater.

The horse's whinny prompted him to go fetch Anna. In reality only a few minutes had passed since he'd taken Emily from the carriage, but in that time they'd covered appreciable subjects. He'd never been around a woman who didn't simper and fawn over him. Emily's practicality made for a refreshing change.

John quietly leaned into the carriage, gently slipped away the fur so he could slide his arms under Anna, and lifted her. Even as he drew her from the dim recesses of the carriage into daylight, she didn't so much as stir.

Lord, have mercy on her. She's been through enough already. He strode toward the house and caught sight through the window of Emily moving about. *Father, while I'm praying, I'll ask You to touch her, too. She's bristly as a brush, but beneath it all, she has a heart of gold. If I can be Your servant to tend these little lambs of Your fold, use me.*

John carried Anna into the bedchamber and quickly noted how Emily hadn't only prepared for her sister to be settled in the bed; she'd also removed the smallest drawer from a bureau. In spite of the chill of the room, Emily had taken off her shawl and folded it to fit the bottom of the drawer. There, in that makeshift bassinet, she now placed the wee babe and smiled at him.

How little it took to make her happy. Before they left the shack that morning, John insisted she finish eating the food Franklin had delivered. She'd relished each bite as if it were a delicacy from the king's own table. Then, too, she subtly saw to it Duncan and Anna received larger shares. She wasn't a woman who put herself first, and that virtue shone through.

John released his small burden and watched as Emily tenderly straightened her sister's limp form, adjusted the blankets in which she was bundled, and added the rest from the bed.

He thought Anna looked ghastly. Had she truly fallen asleep, or was she in a deep swoon? Never had he seen anyone so weak. He no longer wondered why Emily took it upon herself to brave the shipyard in search of the man she thought was Edward. It no longer seemed a foolhardy venture—it had been a move of sheer desperation. John determined he'd send for Dr. Quisinby at once. Something was dreadfully wrong.

Lovingly, Emily smoothed back strands of her sister's hair. "Our dear Lord Jesus, please let this be the start of her coming back to health." Emily then turned to face John. A sweet smile lifted her lips. "She looks so warm and peaceful."

John felt like an intruder, watching that tender moment of hope and devotion. He had some thinking to do. Emily prayed and cherished her Bible. Was it possible his brother had deceived these women? No. John shook his head to dislodge that ridiculous, stray thought. He simply couldn't imagine it. As soon as the *Cormorant* docked, he'd bring Edward here. With Anna and Emily's description, Edward would undoubtedly be able to identify the sailor who bore responsibility.

Time would reveal the truth to these women. Even then, John decided he'd set them up as assistants to a haberdasher or seamstress and settle their little family into a cottage somewhere. He turned to be sure the babe was safe, then mentioned, "I noticed a few logs in the grate."

"Ah, then tonight we'll be snug as—"

"Not tonight—now. I'll see to it you have wood and coal aplenty. Food, too."

"Oh, Mr. Newcomb, you're too kind!" Emily went to the brick fireplace and got down on her knees. Her features pulled with each step, but she gave no complaint. She worked deftly to light the kindling beneath the trio of small logs and said over her shoulder, "I'll be glad to work—to be sure, I'll not be earning whatever it takes to live in such grand style, but I'd like to do my best. Duncan and I—we're just riding coattails, being here. Edward never promised us anything—just Anna."

He chafed at her words. Since he held out no expectation his brother was involved with Anna, he wanted to make sure Emily grasped how things stood. "Until Edward returns, we'll keep to this arrangement. In the meantime, none of you is to mention him."

She turned so quickly, she landed on her backside. Mouth agape, she stared for a moment. A look of utter betrayal altered her features. "Oh, Mr. Newcomb. You tricked me."

"I did nothing of the sort."

"Aye, you did. You brought us to a palace and promised every creaturely comfort. You won Duncan's allegiance by the promise of working with your animals, and my sister and her son will flourish instead of struggle. You said until Edward returned, you'd assume responsibility. I must have been a fool to think you changed your mind, but when you said that, I truly thought you'd reconsidered and were admitting Edward and Anna were wed."

"Now, Emily—"

"I was wrong to allow you to bring us here." Her voice shook, but he couldn't tell if it was with outrage or anguish. "Soon as Anna wakes, we'll go back—"

"No!" The word burst from him; then he cast a glance to be sure he'd not awakened Anna. He scowled back at Emily. "Look at her! You can't possibly last there another day. You're staying put."

She said in a sick hush, "You didn't tell us the cost of coming with you was Anna's dignity and our silence. You lured us here, but now you instruct us to live a lie."

"By staying silent, you're not living a lie, Emily. That marriage license is a fake."

To his horror, tears welled up in her green, green eyes, turning them into pools of infinite suffering. Until now she'd shouldered everything without weeping. He somehow had deluded himself into believing she was too strong to indulge in such feminine weakness. A solitary tear streaked down one pale, gaunt cheek.

Compassion tugged at him, but he needed to be careful. This was a temporary arrangement—until Edward made an appearance and things were resolved or the investigator turned up the real "Edward Newcomb" responsible for devastating these women. John reasoned softly, "You can live quietly here. Anna will recover nicely, and the babe will thrive. Surely you must admit that is more important than any other consideration. You're too tired to think this through. After you sleep a bit, it will all make perfect sense."

She shook her head sadly. "The only thing I know is, I've taken cookies from the devil's own kitchen."

seven

Bone weary as she felt, Emily's turmoil kept her from resting. Once Mr. Newcomb left, she turned to her brother. "We've got work to do, Boy-o."

He sneezed, then laughed. "It's dusty in here."

"Aye, that it is. Scare up a broom. I'll knock down the cobwebs and sweep the walls and floor." She looked at the maize-colored drapery. "Do you think you could shove a chair over to the walls and scramble up it so as to take down the curtains?"

His wee chest puffed out 'til he looked like a proud little robin that just gobbled the longest worm in the park. "There's no doubt about it. I'll pull down every last one of them—just watch if I don't."

"I'm sure you can. Then we'll take them out and drape them on the hedges. You can beat them, and the wind will blow the rest of the dust out 'til they come clean enough. Now let's get to it." She made a shooing motion with her hands. "Find me a broom."

They got busy. No stranger to cleaning, Emily organized herself and efficiently rid the cottage of the depressing air of disuse. How could anyone neglect such a palace?

Her ankle hurt, but she'd learned to kneel on the seat of a chair to keep the weight off her ankle when the twinges got too bad. The chair could move about the room with her so she was able to keep working. She swept down everything once, then pulled the covers off the furniture. A collection of treasures lay hidden beneath those covers—a golden velvet settee, a rose-and-gold-striped wingbacked chair, two charming little nesting tables, an oak rocking chair, and a petit point footstool featuring a cabbage rose pattern.

Emily couldn't contain her delight over each piece as Duncan folded in the cloth to uncover it. "Oh, now, can't you just imagine our Anna, holding her babe in that rocker?"

Duncan rapped his knuckles on the smaller table. "Aye, and this is just the right size for me!"

The dust from the covers they removed made it necessary to sweep the floor yet again, but Duncan obliged. After that, they each took a wet rag and mopped the wooden floorboards until they gleamed.

Duncan found a crock of vinegar in the pantry and a bucket in the alcove. He sloshed water on the windows from the outside, and she used diluted vinegar on the inside of them so the sun could shine through.

Twice Emily stopped to help Anna with the babe. When she came back after the second episode, she sat down in a chair for just a second.

&

"What in the world?" John squinted at the hedges. His brows knit. "Surely she didn't—"

Oh, but she had. The cottage's curtains flapped in the stiff noonday breeze like semaphores on a clipper. He dismounted from his prized bay and blazed right through the open door. Once inside, he stopped in his tracks. Duncan sat cross-legged on a spotless floor over by the window, crooning softly to the babe in his lap.

Sunlight flooded the cottage from the sparkling clean, curtainless windows, giving a cheerful air to the furnishings they'd uncovered. Hard work and devout prayer together shouldn't have accomplished half of the miracle he saw.

That hard work—and probably the prayer, too, he admitted

to himself—came from one very young woman. Her temple rested against the wing of a rose-and-gold-striped chair. Dirt streaked her face and smudged her muslin apron. The cuffs of her dress remained turned up, as if she'd awaken any moment and resume what must have been a frantic pace of labor. Her bosom rose and fell in the slow rhythm of sleep. After slaving for Wilkens, John marveled she'd stayed awake long enough to do anything at all. He glanced about the cottage once more, then looked at her and decided on a course of action.

"Our Em is sore tired," Duncan whispered. "Anna says we must let her sleep."

"Not there. She looks horribly uncomfortable."

"I emptied our belongings from my blanket, Sir. We can cover her."

John cast a look at the bedchamber, then thought better of carrying Emily to it. There was no telling what state Anna was in. He'd do better using the settee as a makeshift bed for this headstrong woman. Earlier he'd wondered what furniture lay beneath the dusty covers and suspected he might have to raid his warehouse to scare up replacement items if the mice had nested in anything. It came as a pleasant surprise to discover things were in good repair.

Emily was a short woman—the settee would accommodate her nicely enough for now. Anna had slept through his moving her. Certainly, as weary as Emily must be, she'd never know if he lifted her and popped her onto the settee. He drew closer and barely made contact, but Emily turned into a raging tigress.

Women, in his experience, were delicate and powerless. Ladylike, they'd never done more than swoon, rap a man's knuckles with a fan, or, even at their boldest, slap his cheek. Emily broke that rule. All four limbs went into action, taking a purposeful defense.

His arms tightened. "Calm yourself!"

❧

From the first day in steerage on the ship, Emily learned she had to protect herself. Working at the asylum only reinforced that fact. The merest touch would send her into a defensive flurry. She kicked with her right foot. A strangled cry tore out of her throat as she arched in anguish. Fire shot through her, then ice. Emily fought to cling to the edges of reality as everything went cold and dark. Someone called her name, but she couldn't answer. For a moment she floated; then there was nothingness.

"Talk to her," she vaguely heard a man say. Someone patted her cheek lightly several times, then ceased that—only to start chaffing her hand. "Emily. Come now, Emily. Wake up." The man's voice sounded quite concerned.

Emily stirred. A single slight shift, and the agony in her ankle mushroomed. Whimpers poured out of her. She bit her lip to silence that sign of weakness.

"Eh, our Emily," Duncan said from a long way off. "You're right fair. Aye, you are. All is well."

She struggled to open her grainy eyes and barely lifted her head. Waves of weariness and pain made her head droop back down. Where was she? It took a moment before she recalled John Newcomb bringing them to this wondrous cottage. . .but how had she come to lie on the settee? Her ankle hurt so badly, she barely managed to choke out, "Duncan?"

John Newcomb's face hovered into view. "Your brother is behind you, tending Anna's babe. Lie still."

"Anna?"

"Fine. She's just fine. In fact, she's probably in better shape than you are." Mr. Newcomb flipped a familiar-looking blanket over her. He seemed angry enough to spit anvils.

Now what have I done?

"The babe smiled at me, Em. I'm certain of it."

She kept her eyes trained on Mr. Newcomb while she whispered in a shaky voice, "Now isn't that sweet, Duncan! Anna's wee one is going to look up to you for love and protection."

"The way Anna and Duncan do to you?" John asked.

"Aye, and fitting it is. I'm. . .the eldest," she answered. Those few words seemed to drain her of most of her energy. She knew it was rude to ignore a guest, but everything wavered around her.

A warm hand curved around her jaw. Someone, somewhere, crooned in a deep, musical baritone to her. He bade her to rest, to sleep. Surely that couldn't be Mr. Newcomb. Her eyelids felt too heavy to lift, so she couldn't prove it; but as angry and mean as he'd been so far, Emily felt sure Lucifer would be wearing snowshoes before John Newcomb ever uttered a kind word to her.

"Things will be easier for you now. Be at peace."

❧

"Emily. Miss O'Brien? Sorry to wake you when you barely got to sleep, but Dr. Quisinby is here."

Emily shook her head to dispel the lethargy grabbing at her. "Yes. Yes, thank you." She started to sit up, but large, strong hands touched her shoulders and pressed her back down into the luxurious, horsehair-stuffed velvet cushion. She blinked to clear away the haze of sleep and focused on none other than John Newcomb. Deep lines furrowed his brow. She murmured, "If you give me a moment, I'll make sure Anna is prepared for him."

"I've already examined your sister," a strange voice said. Emily looked past John Newcomb and spied an old, bewhiskered man dressed in a somber, charcoal gray jacket. Gold buttons on the garment hinted he conducted a very successful practice. Indeed, it didn't strain her mind in the least to believe him to be accomplished in his profession. Just his appearance inspired confidence in his ability. He studied her sternly but said nothing more.

His very silence alarmed her. "How is Anna? What about the baby?"

"We'll discuss that after the doctor examines you. Duncan and I will absent ourselves for a short while." John rose, and Emily belatedly realized he'd been kneeling at her side. He waggled his finger at her. "You cooperate. No more of your foolish stubbornness. Come, Duncan." He reached his hand around her brother's shoulder and led him out the door.

Emily started to sit up yet again, but Dr. Quisinby's stern look made her lie back down.

"Let's not put up any pretenses, Miss. Anyone who could sleep through the wailing that babe was making must be suffering extreme exhaustion. Stay where you are, and I'll make this as simple as possible."

The front door closed, and Emily flashed what she hoped looked like a confident smile at the doctor. "Sir, I truly appreciate how you saw to my sister. I don't need—"

He held up a hand, as if to silence her. His features altered into a scowl. "Mr. Newcomb was excessively clear in his directive."

Unable to refute that assertion, Emily resorted to the humiliating truth. "I understand his concern, Doctor"—she felt her face flame—"but I don't have a single coin in my pocket. It'll take me a long while to pay you back for seeing to my Anna."

He stepped closer and started to peel away the blanket. "You needn't fret over that. Mr. Newcomb already saw to my fee. He warned me you'd likely try to beg off. Furthermore, he garnered my pledge to persist. Now that that's settled, I may as well have a look—"

Emily endured the embarrassing questions and answered

them as best she could while trying to preserve her dignity, but when he reached for her ankle, she tensed. No woman of decency—however rich or poor—permitted a man to view or touch such scandalous portions of her being.

"Miss O'Brien, it's obvious you've injured yourself. Mr. Newcomb is most concerned. He informed me you've hurt your limb quite badly and fell into a deep swoon today. You must be practical enough to allow me to assess the extent of the damage and treat you." The doctor's austere expression reinforced his opinion.

Planning to protest, Emily drew in a breath but exhaled without saying a word. Whatever argument she made would either sound foolish or be a falsehood.

"It would be an ill-considered move to refuse my assistance, since an injury of this nature could very likely cause you to collapse while you're carrying your nephew. Even if that didn't happen, you might well end up lame if this is broken. Then what help will you be to your sister?"

Emily grudgingly accepted the truth of his words. She compressed her lips and nodded. When the doctor took her calf into his hands, she nearly shot off the settee. As he started to unwind the cloth she'd used to bind her ankle, the swelling and discoloration became apparent. Emily had tried her best to keep Duncan and Anna from seeing the sad condition of her limb. When Mr. Newcomb accidentally saw it last night because he'd boldly let himself into their home, she'd nearly been embarrassed out of her skin.

"Yes, then, this looks quite sore," the doctor murmured in a sympathetic tone as he peered over his spectacles at her.

Emily feared she would be violently ill when he set aside the cloth and lightly ran his fingers over the beginning of the bruise above her ankle. She swallowed the bile, but he tightened his hold and began to turn the joint. The pain exploded.

"Just leave the cloth over her brow." A deep murmur reached through the haze. "I'd rather not use hartshorn and revive her until I have this bound."

Emily forced her lids to flutter open. It took half of forever before she could remove the soggy handkerchief from her forehead or form any words, and even then they sounded faint. "Forgive me. . . . I'm not usually. . .this giddy."

"My estimation is, you're normally a stalwart soul," the doctor said. He took a glass of water from Duncan and added a few drops of something to it. "Drink this."

She evaded the rim of the glass. "What is it?"

"Laudanum."

"Oh, Doctor, no. I don't think—"

"Don't quibble, Emily." She twisted a bit and realized John Newcomb was back. His dark countenance made her worry about what else had upset him. "Drink the stuff. You're not a brave little soldier; you're a hurting woman."

The doctor's whiskers spread apart as he grinned. "If you were a brave soldier, you'd be demanding a stiff whiskey."

Emily started to curl and set her elbow and hand on the settee to help push herself upright. Weak as she felt, she didn't mind John's silent assistance. He smoothly sat her up, then braced her as she fought a wave of dizziness. The men exchanged a few words, but Emily couldn't quite distinguish them. Everything sounded muffled and far away.

"Here." John Newcomb's voice registered. So did the sensation of something pressed against her lips.

Emily opened her eyes again. At least the dizziness had passed.

"Drink it. Come now, Emily. Every last drop."

She gave him a wry look but obeyed. For smelling so sweet, the contents of the cup tasted acrid. She suppressed a shudder. "How is Anna?"

"She's weak and malnourished," the doctor stated baldly. "Her milk is coming in, but she'll have to eat like a horse to build up a good supply."

"That won't be a problem," John stated crisply as he handed the cup to Duncan and pointed toward the kitchen drainboard in a silent order to set it out of the way.

"She told me you've been brewing fenugreek tea for her," the doctor said. "That's precisely what I prescribe to increase milk, so you're to continue to give it to her thrice daily."

"Otherwise—" Emily cast an embarrassed look at John as he took a seat in the striped wingback chair she'd fallen asleep in a short while earlier. She then focused back on the doctor as she lowered her voice to a flustered whisper. "Is Anna going to fare well?"

"From the looks of things, she suffered through a difficult birthing."

"The midwife said as much."

Dr. Quisinby let out a small huff of air. His face and tone held a hint of sadness. "Judging from her condition and comparing it to my previous cases, I anticipate hers will be a lengthy recovery. In truth, you'd best prepare her gently for the fact that this son will be her only child."

Emily bit the inside of her cheek to hold back her reaction. Part of her wanted to scream at the injustice. The other part wondered if God had done this to save Anna from further humiliation since she was already a shunned wife.

"Her blood needs to be built back up," the doctor continued.

Emily nodded. Fretting over truth never changed the fact. Best she keep her mind set on the things that would make a difference and leave the rest to the Almighty. God would get them through. "Just tell me what my sister needs. I'll do whatever you instruct."

"Plenty of sleep for both of you ladies. Generous portions

of decent food to regain some strength."

"I'll have my cook see to them," John said. "What do you suggest?"

"Beef. Buttermilk. Egg custards and the like. Your cook is redoubtable—set the situation before her, and she'll see to matters." The doctor rummaged in a black leather satchel and produced a tall, square bottle. "This tonic should work nicely. Nasty-tasting, of course, but the best ones tend to be that way. All three of you are to take a spoonful each morning."

Emily eyed the bottle. *If I don't take any, it'll last—*

John Newcomb leaned forward and rasped, "I don't like the calculating look in your eye, Emily O'Brien. You're not going to forego your own doses so Duncan and Anna have more."

Emily felt her cheeks grow hot with guilt.

"Do I have your word?" John folded his arms across his chest and stared at her.

Grudgingly, Emily nodded. "Aye, 'tis my word you have."

John gestured toward her ankle. "Is it broken?"

"Badly sprained," Dr. Quisinby said. "Very badly sprained. Pity of it is, sprains can take longer than a break to heal. She needs to keep off it. No gadding about."

John rose. He shook the doctor's hand. "I thank you for coming." He escorted the doctor out. Emily slumped into the corner of the settee. Minutes later, the echo of John Newcomb's fine knee boots on the wooden floor made her open her eyes.

"Here." A damp cloth draped from his fingertips.

"I'm thanking you," she whispered as she took the cloth and lifted it in both hands to bury her face in it. The spicy scent clinging to the cloth registered as both foreign and comforting. She inhaled deeply and proceeded to wash her face and hands. "Aye, I'm thanking you, John Newcomb, for seeing to my dear ones. Duncan and my Anna have suffered terribly. I'm ever so grate—"

"Hush." He whisked away the cloth and shoved a plate into her hands.

She whispered a prayer, then silently ate the slice of cold roasted beef, a dried fig, and a small chunk of bread and drank a bit of pomegranate juice. "Oh, that was a fine feast."

"How is your, ah, foot feeling?"

Such a gentleman. Even if she was just a dirt-poor immigrant, he'd not mentioned her ankle. "It's much better, thank you." Emily manufactured a grateful smile as she looked at him. Both of him.

He took the plate from her hand and set it down on a nearby table. "You ought to sleep quite soundly now that the laudanum is starting to work."

"Anna—"

"Young though he is, Duncan is quite adept at assisting her." John fleetingly touched her cheek, and her heavy lids fluttered shut.

For the first time in years, she felt safe. Gratitude and relief flooded her.

"Emily, I'm going to carry you to your bed."

She forced herself to look at him again. "No, thank you." She patted the arm of the settee. "Sleep here. . .don't want"— she blinked—"bother Anna."

"As you wish."

The room started to melt sideways; then Emily realized it was because John had somehow moved her to the center of the settee. "Lie down, little one." He coaxed her to tilt back, then guided her shoulders onto the inviting seat cushions.

"That's the way of it," he praised in a croon as he lifted her limbs and tucked them onto the seat. Even muzzy as her mind felt, Emily knew he took great care not to bump her ankle.

"But the ba—"

"Stop fretting and sleep." He took the blankets he'd used

earlier to cover her and draped them gently over her and tucked them about her shoulders. "Do you want a pillow?"

She sighed in pure bliss and shook her head. She'd been sitting by Anna's bed to sleep for so long that just lying down on something soft and having her own blanket felt like heaven on earth. Anna could keep the fine feather pillows. As the fingers of sleep reached for her, Emily remembered to mumble, "Thank you for everything."

≈

A few days later, the vicar paid a call. His arrival came as no surprise since Emily had asked John if he could send word to the vicar that they'd welcome a visit.

She'd been too worried to leave Anna and the babe alone for the few hours it would have taken to go to church. Indeed, she missed going to worship something fierce; but since she'd taken over both jobs at the asylum, she'd been unable to attend.

Emily consoled herself with the knowledge that this was only a temporary situation and God had promised to be with her at all times. John Newcomb had entered their lives and displayed such generosity and kindness to Anna and Duncan—a fact that Emily counted as proof God still hovered close enough to hear and answer her constant prayers.

Duncan was off at the stables, and Anna lay napping soundly on the wondrously soft, big bed when the vicar arrived. For the first few moments, Emily fought with herself. Edward had brought along what might well have been a man simply posing as a parson. Could John Newcomb have taken a page out of that copybook and done the same thing? She knew she could put her trust in God; putting it in man was another issue entirely.

Emily invited the vicar to have a seat and tried to carry on polite small talk. Instead of plowing to the heart of the matter, he pleasantly carried the conversation, invited her to attend church, and spoke of how the choir would begin practice for the Advent services soon. His kindly concern and gentle spirit proved him to be a true man of the cloth. Swallowing her pride, Emily told him of their predicament.

"Well, now, why don't you show me the marriage certificate?"

She reverently took out the parchment and prayed ever so hard he'd tell her all was well. When Edward and the priest brought the certificate with them, she and Anna were thrilled with it. It wasn't simple paper—no, 'twas made of fine parchment, and the words were scripted on it in a fine hand. Roses crowned the top of a gold-embossed square that framed the whole affair, and she and Anna had been careful to sign their names on the lines with their very best penmanship. John's comment about Edward's signature rang true, though—'twas little more than a scribble.

The vicar accepted the page and carried it over to the window so he could read the script more easily. Clouds were rolling in so even that light seemed questionable.

"I'll fetch a lamp."

"No need, no need," he murmured.

Emily watched as his lips moved in silent reading. She couldn't determine any particular reaction. Finally he looked up. "Child, I'm sorry to tell you this is no marriage license. Someone went to a bit of trouble to create a beautiful imitation, but that's what this is: a counterfeit. It holds just enough liturgical words to fool someone who doesn't read Latin, but most of it is sheer babble."

Emily pressed her palm to her mouth to hold back a scream. Rage pulsed through her.

"Now, then, it's a crying pity."

"It's more than a pity—'tis a crime!" She wound her arms around her ribs. "I never suspected he was a scoundrel. He courted our Anna and charmed us all. When he brought the priest, I trusted that a man of God wouldn't do something amiss." She cast a horrified look at the bedchamber door, then looked back at him. Until now she'd hoped all of this was a case of John Newcomb's simply being wrong.

The full reality hit, and Emily knew she couldn't deny the awful truth any longer. "Poor Anna! Oh, my poor sister! What are we to do?"

"There's nothing to be done," the priest answered gently. "Some things in life you set behind you. Much as it pains me to speak the truth and even more pained as you'll be to hear it, this will have to be one of them you not only set behind you, but close the door on. As far as I can see, there's only one hope. John Newcomb is a righteous man. If the Edward Newcomb who signed this is John's brother, you can count on John to rectify the matter."

The fraudulent wedding parchment crackled as he set it aside. After a time of thick silence, he shook his head sadly. "The past is the past. We must now deal with the present. Why don't you bring the babe to me?"

Emily smiled at him gratefully. "Even if the marriage isn't real, you're willing to acknowledge him?"

"Every child deserves to be welcomed into the world. I'd be honored to pray for the boy. Perhaps, given the circumstances, it would be best if we simply tended my giving a blessing here." The kindly old man gave her a sad, aching smile. "With your sister ailing, I'm sure she'll find peace, knowing we'll love and accept her son."

Indeed, that is precisely what they did. Emily served the priest tea until Duncan came home and Anna woke. Because Anna couldn't move without hurting, Emily went into the bedchamber and opened the curtains and windows so she wouldn't feel as if the visit were being conducted under cover of dark and shame. The damp smell of coming rain filled the room. She hastily combed and braided Anna's hair and tried very gently to let her sister know the vicar had confirmed John Newcomb's evaluation of the wedding parchment.

Anna's pretty eyes filled with tears, but she didn't say a word.

"Ach, now. You know Duncan and I love you. We know you didn't do a thing wrong, and the vicar said the selfsame thing. I'm supposing we could spend all of eternity being upset, but that won't change a thing. You have a babe—a sweet one at that. We love him dearly—all of us."

Anna cradled the little one closer to her bosom. She choked back her tears and agreed weakly, "Aye, we do."

"So let's forget entertaining regrets and make sure he grows up to be a young man who follows the Lord." Emily then gave the baby a quick swipe with a damp towel, popped him into a fresh nappy, and wrapped him in her own shawl.

"Are we ready?" Duncan asked from the doorway.

"Aye, I'm supposing we are," Anna answered in a hushed voice.

The vicar and Duncan came in. As they did, the clouds in the sky blocked out the weak sun. The vicar peeped at the babe, gave Anna a few kind words for herself, and exclaimed over what a fine child she'd borne, then took out a prayer book. Though she'd heard the words before, Emily listened even more closely this time. It was so very precious, having someone speak to the Lord about this beloved little child. The vicar paused briefly. "What name have you given him?"

A moment later, he repeated the name Anna tearfully decided upon. The skies opened up, and all heaven cried for the travesty.

eight

"Very good, Duncan!"

Duncan beamed and clutched the edges of the slate. He turned it so Anna could appreciate his work, too. "See? I knew that one, too!"

"Oh, now, aren't you a smart lad," Anna praised.

Emily had found a slate tucked beneath a stack of moldy books. Ever since Anna had started having trouble carrying the babe, they'd stopped giving Duncan his lessons. They'd gladly plunged back into them, and the slate made it all that much easier.

"Give me another one," Duncan begged.

"Hmm." Emily closed her Bible, then opened it. Her finger landed in the upper third of the page. She started to giggle.

"What's so funny?" Anna asked.

"Yes, please do tell me. What's so funny?" John asked. He leaned on the bedroom window and peeked inside. He grinned. "I don't mean to invade your privacy, but I don't believe I've ever heard Emily laugh before. I had to see if my ears were playing tricks on me."

"Oh, it's our Em, all right," Duncan said. He galloped over to the window and held up the slate. "We're playing a game. Em finds a verse in the Bible, and I'm to copy as many words out of it as I can spell correctly."

"There's a novel game." John looked at the slate, then reached in and rumpled Duncan's hair. "You did a fine job on that one. I still don't see why Emily laughed, though."

"Neither do we," Anna agreed. "What's so funny, Em?"

Emily looked back down at her Bible and spluttered into laughter again. "You'll never believe this," she warned. Her eyes shimmered with glee.

"I'm ready," Duncan declared as he poised the stylus over the slate. "Try me!"

" 'Jesus wept.' "

John watched through the window as Duncan's face twisted with confusion. Anna started to giggle, and Emily set aside the Bible and dissolved into hilarity. His own laughter boomed in, though it was more a result of the pure joy of seeing them all happy than at the fact that she'd happened to give her little brother such a simple verse.

Duncan set aside his slate, propped his chin on the windowsill, and asked in a bewildered tone, "Why are you all laughing when it says Jesus was crying?"

John grabbed him, dragged him through the wide-open window, and flipped him upside down. He playfully shook the lad until he laughed, then set him on his feet. "We laughed because Em wanted to stump a smart boy like you with a hard verse, and the best she could do was give you two little words."

"Em's a giggle box today."

"Oh, she is, is she?"

"Uh-huh." Duncan led him into the house and straight into the bedchamber, where Anna and Emily still battled to subdue their chuckles.

John watched Emily try to paste on a serene expression, but her lips twitched a bit. He wanted to start laughing all over again, too. He gave her arm a quick squeeze, then winked at Anna. Autumn sunlight filled the room, and the day seemed far more golden and warm than the calendar dictated. "So what set you into this jolly mood?"

"I'm afraid I started it. My pillow got a wee hole in it last night. I woke up wearing feathers in my hair," Emily began.

"And Anna said she looked like a loon," Duncan added.

"Then the baby got the hiccups," Emily said.

"And I got a funny, brown mustache from drinking the hot chocolate," Anna confessed sheepishly.

"Duncan somehow accidentally got a nappy tucked into his waist and walked about like he had a tail for ever so long before he realized it," Emily said, her voice quivering with laughter. "And then he spelled 'beloved' as 'B-loved'!"

John belted out a laugh. "You're having quite a silly day!"

"So it's your turn. What have you done today?" Duncan asked.

John simply couldn't let the delight of the day fizzle just because he didn't have a confession to make. He theatrically tapped one finger on his chin, then shrugged. "I don't know. I'm having an ordinary day. I can't think of a single, solitary thing that's happened to me that warrants any laughter at all." Just as he finished speaking, he sat on the edge of a chair and let his elbow bump the side table so he'd have to bobble to catch the flower vase he'd upset. The laughter in the room was ample reward for his intentional clumsiness.

Soon the gaiety extended to their playing tic-tac-toe on the slate. Instead of using O and X marks, they drew pictures of animals. "Your cat looks more like a rat," Emily told John.

He gave her an exaggerated look of offense. "You had to tell me yours was a bear. I thought it was a monkey!"

"It didn't have a long tail," Emily retorted. She turned to Anna. "Tell him I drew a grand bear."

Anna's eyes grew wide with poorly feigned innocence. "Oh, that was a bear? I thought 'twas a snowman with ear muffs."

"Fat lot you know," Emily teased back. "Your snake looked more like a worm than anything else."

The merriment continued. John deeply regretted having to leave for a meeting. He'd seen the O'Briens somber far too much. This slice of time came as a complete surprise—and a delightful one, at that.

Adding to his relief, Duncan, Anna, and Emily had observed his one stricture: They didn't mention Edward's name in their discussions when others were present. Now that he thought of it, they didn't even mention his brother in his presence, either. Whether 'twas out of embarrassment or obedience, he didn't know. The simple fact that Edward's name remained unspoken and his honor and reputation were spared satisfied John.

When the situation warranted some form of reference, Anna simply said, "My husband." From that, everyone held the impression that she must be the wife of one of the shipping company's new captains—a false deduction John neither denied nor confirmed. As far as things went, the situation continued to unfold far more amiably than he'd expected.

"I'll have to look around the house," he said as he left. "I recall a cribbage board."

"Oh, that would be fine," Anna smiled.

"And Duncan could speed up on doing his sums by counting the hands," Emily chimed in.

"Do you play chess?"

Emily's brows knit. John had a wild urge to reach over and smooth the furrows with a gentle stroke of his finger. Instead he clasped his hands behind his back and listened as she said, "That's far too fancy a game for us simple folk, Mr. Newcomb."

He winked, then gave her a look of mock severity. "Miss O'Brien, no one can be terrible at everything in life. I've seen how you can draw. Surely your ability to play chess would have to be an improvement. Anything would be an improvement!"

"I think I've been insulted," Emily groused.

"Oh, no. Not in the least," Anna twittered. "Mr. Newcomb was trying to express his faith in your ability to learn the game of kings."

"Kings are boys," Duncan said. "If it's a boys' game, maybe Mr. Newcomb had better teach it to me instead."

"We'll make a date of it. I'll bring cookies and milk tonight after supper. I'll teach you all how to play chess," John promised.

Duncan started to chortle. "Oh, now you know what our Em will say about that!"

"No, I don't. What will Em say?" John's brows hiked as he looked to Emily.

Emily shrugged.

"Remember what I told you once before? Em used to tell me that God brings meat; the devil brings cookies!"

"Duncan!" Emily gasped. Her cheeks went bright red—as red as the peppermint sticks John had decided to bring that night.

❧

A few days later, Dr. Quisinby dropped in. After he examined Anna, he sat down to have some coffee with Emily. "Between that tonic and eating well, you and Duncan are looking far better."

Something in his tone made Emily stop cold. She set down her cup and stared at him in dread. "Anna—?"

"She's not recovering, Emily."

"What shall I do? Does she need other medicine? Should I—"

"Emily," he broke in. He shook his head sadly. "I had my suspicions when I saw her the first time. This visit merely confirmed them."

"You have to be wrong. She has a babe. A son needs his ma. Surely there's something—" When he shook his head again, Emily propped her elbows on the tabletop and buried her face in her hands. "I should have—"

"No," he interrupted. "She told me she was sick the last three months of carrying the baby."

"If she'd eaten more, stayed warm—"

He rose and came around the table and pulled her to face him. "Emily, none of that would have made the difference. I have rich, fat women who suffer this same malady. My medical text discusses it, but there is no cure. There is no blame to assume, no situation to second guess."

"I don't want Anna to know. I don't want her to worry about little Timmy."

Dr. Quisinby nodded. "I concur. Let her last days be happy ones."

"Duncan—I don't want him told, either."

"As you wish. Perhaps 'twould be wise to let Mr. Newcomb know. Would you like me to inform him?"

Emily nodded. The doctor and room blurred as the reality sank in and tears started to flow.

❧

"Of all of the idiotic things in the world!" John roared. He lengthened his stride and hastened toward the small cottage as he served Emily his hottest glower. She stood in the doorway, her arms wrapped about her sister. The two of them looked ready to topple over any second.

John wedged himself between Anna and the doorframe, then swept her into his arms. Weak as she was, she melted against him like a candle accidentally left out in the sun. Appalled at the thought that they'd have both tumbled down the steps if he'd not happened along, he locked eyes with Emily. "Just what do you think you're doing, letting her get out of bed?"

"Anna was wanting some sunshine," Emily explained as she allowed him to hold the load she'd been struggling with.

She tugged the hem of Anna's nightgown down to cover her limbs. "You cannot blame her—she's been inside for nigh unto three months."

"If she falls, she'll spend centuries in a pine box until the eternal trump sounds!" John was horrified by this whole turn of events. Emily's stricken look let him know he'd almost spilled the truth. Regret swamped him. He immediately softened his tone. "Forgive me. I'm complaining for no good reason. Here. Let me help."

In the recesses of his mind, he couldn't be sure whether he worried more about Emily or Anna, though. Neither of them was in any condition to endure the slightest exertion, let alone a tumble. Though rest and decent meals had perked up Emily, she had no business half-carrying Anna when she still limped.

Dr. Quisinby spoke circumspectly, but his message came through clearly. Anna had little time left, and Emily—John gritted his teeth. The way she'd swooned the day he brought them to the cottage alarmed him. In those moments he'd finally seen beyond her fiercely brave façade to how truly weak, thin, and ragged she'd become. He'd held her in his arms and known for the first time a wave of inexplicable protectiveness. At that moment he'd determined to do whatever it took to shield and care for this woman.

Quisinby confirmed his suspicions when he'd said Emily undoubtedly gave her own portion of food to her sister and suffered hunger out of the selfless hope that Anna and the babe would fare better due to her sacrifice.

Even when she'd been sagging from exhaustion, Emily had clung to his kerchief and tried with touching sincerity to thank him for all he'd done for her brother and sister's suffering—and never once confessed she'd been even more hungry and cold than they. Aye, and even as he'd tucked her in on that settee, her last thoughts had been of the baby and another vague whisper of thanks. He'd bent forward and taken up the kerchief again. The generous dose of laudanum the good doctor had given her kept her placid as John dabbed one last smudge from her temple.

Now he wished he could wipe away the worried look in her eyes just as easily. Keeping the secret from Anna had to be so very hard on her. To his astonishment, Emily hid this burden just as she'd hidden her hunger and thinness. To look at her quick smile and listen to her cheerful talk, anyone would guess she didn't have a trouble in the world.

Over the last week, John thought to stay away from the small cottage. It wasn't easy—in fact, it rated as impossible. Every day something essential gave him cause to stop by. While there, he sought signs that the sisters were resting and eating well. He'd ordered his cook over at the main house to send down hearty meals thrice a day. The place looked tidy as a spinster's parlor, and the tray of washed dishes bore mute testimony to the fact that the O'Briens were eating adequately.

At times John found himself wandering through the warehouse at the shipping yard to find things to deliver to them as an excuse to check in again each evening. For the first time since he'd taken command of Newcomb Shipping, he'd found his mind straying off business and onto the welfare of Emily's family. He'd never thought much of the fripperies that went out in the spare spaces of his vessels, but those caused him every bit as much happiness as they did for the O'Briens. Knowing how Emily felt about charity, he made it a point to have his cook leave the teapot and tea. He left the ball after tossing it with Duncan—stating they'd play with it again. Indeed they did—both for a good excuse for him to return as well as the fact that playing with the lad was fun.

Then, too, there was something uniquely delightful about the O'Briens. In the midst of all their trials, Emily and Anna still found reasons to laugh. It seemed like the very sunshine of their love held back the cold season. Indeed, by sheer force of her will, Emily kept Anna blissfully comfortable and ignorant. Due to Emily's imaginative ideas, energy, and determination, John felt certain the caretaker's cottage had never contained so much love and laughter.

Until now.

He'd just groused at them and spoiled their joyful anticipation of this insignificant outing. He let out a sigh. "When the doctor wants her out of bed, at least be sure I'm here to help."

Anna barely pressed her hand on his shoulder. "Oh, please don't be cross with us. Dr. Quisinby paid a visitation here today, Sir. When I asked, he said I could be in the sun if there was no breeze."

"Most likely he thought you'd have the sense to sit by a sunny window, not come parading outside."

"Oh." Anna's face drooped with dismay.

John felt ten times an ogre. He'd been in a sickbed a few times and recalled how he'd chafed to be up and about after only a day or two. Other than the carriage ride here, Anna hadn't been outside in ages. Indeed, she'd never again feel the kiss of a breeze or the glow of the sun unless they gave her that chance now. She may as well relish those simple pleasures one last time. He held her a bit more securely and grumbled, "Did your sister at least have the presence of mind to bring a chair out here and set it someplace secluded?"

Emily shot him an offended look. "Follow me, please."

Her stiff-backed posture would have amused him had she not seemed so very vulnerable. Emily O'Brien possessed a temper every bit as fiery as her hair, and it gave her a deceptive air of strength. He'd learned now to look beyond the façade she built so carefully and hid behind—but he wondered at times whether that was for her siblings' benefit or if she'd constructed it to mute the impact of life's unrelenting and unmerciful blows.

She was a woman of contradictions. The somber face she showed others and the simple joys she found with her family were like night and day. The joy of the Lord shone from her, in her tender loving care and sweet laughter—but those moments stayed only within the walls of their home. How very sad she found it necessary to wear that cloak of wariness with others. It was as if she were hiding her light under a bushel—but because she feared the wind would blow it out.

As she crossed the well-manicured lawn, his eyes narrowed when he noticed her uneven gait. It bothered him, knowing she'd injured herself in his shipyard. Just because she endured without complaining didn't mean she still wasn't suffering. If he'd come to realize anything at all, it was that Emily O'Brien wouldn't ask for a scrap of attention or a bit of care for herself—even if she were in dire need. At first he thought pride kept her from it; but over the last days, he'd come to see she was a rare soul—one who simply loved others so deeply that she discounted her own needs as unimportant. He cleared his throat to garner her attention, but since she failed to take that cue, he called, "Emily?"

She paused and looked over her shoulder. "Aye?"

He strove to keep his voice mild. "You should still use the walking stick. Where is it?"

"I haven't the slightest notion." She started hobbling again. "I set it aside two days ago. It slows me down far too much."

John opened his mouth to command her to find and use it, but he quelled the impulse. He'd take up the matter out of Anna's hearing. Emily did her utmost to make sure her sister had nothing more to trouble her, and he agreed with that merciful decision. Emily's judgment on what her siblings needed had yet to be anything other than right on the mark.

"Duncan was playing with her walking stick last night," Anna said. "He pretended it was one of your beautiful horses. He kept himself busy, riding back and forth across the bedchamber. I don't know where he set the cane when he grew tired."

"It doesn't matter," Emily replied blithely.

John paused for a moment when he rounded a hedge and reached the side of the house. Over at the edge of the yard, Emily had formed a little haven for her sister. The location was exceedingly clever. It caught the warm sun yet claimed the nestling shelter of being in the crook where the hedges formed a corner. A small box rested in front of the wicker chair—waiting to support Anna's feet. Off to the side, Emily left what looked to be a picnic basket. In a crock she'd even gathered up a fistful of, well, flowery-leafy things. He'd never bothered to learn the names of plants, but the collection of color-changed leaves and dried-out stalks looked quite handsome.

John marveled at Emily's ability to turn what little she had into someplace so inviting. She'd done it here in the yard, just as she'd scrubbed the cottage until it sparkled. Even that dreadful shanty had been neat as a pin, and she'd hidden the newspaper insulating its window with a colorful bit of cloth. There was something novel and admirable about a woman who found contentment so easily. Emily relished simple sunshine and a tiny, plain cottage.

Emily patted the chair. "Now here you are, our Anna-dear. Won't you have a grand time, turning your pretty face to the dear Lord's sun?"

"That I will."

After he settled Anna in her place, John straightened up and studied her for a moment. "Are you warm enough?"

She self-consciously gathered her shawl about her thin shoulders. "Aye. Thank you for asking. Would you care to join us? We're about to have nooning."

He didn't feel the least bit hungry, yet he nodded. "I'd be delighted to join you. Thank you for the invitation."

Emily murmured something unintelligible, then hastened back into the cottage and returned with the baby. John stood by Anna's side and took pains to be sure he didn't block the sun so she'd benefit from its meager warmth. He looked at the new mother and wondered aloud, "You know, I'm so used to hearing you call him the babe or man-child, I don't recall ever hearing the little one's proper name. So tell me, Anna, what are you calling your son?"

Anna's gaze dropped. In a heartbroken whisper, she answered, "Timothy Edward O'Brien."

Emily slipped her bundled nephew into Anna's arms. As she turned away, John saw how tears started to fill her eyes. He'd expected Anna to mention only a first name—not a full name. The ache in her voice made his guts clench, and he knew Emily heard it as well. He cleared his throat. "Timothy is a fine name for a boy. Strong. A fine man in the Holy Bible, too."

Anna refused to look up. She protectively fussed with the blanket to be sure the babe's ears were covered. She avoided any eye contact as she said, "Mr. Newcomb, I thank you for your care. As soon as Em and I can arrange employment and housing, we'll be leaving."

nine

"That's not necessary!" John stared at them in horror.

Emily drew close and set her hand on Anna's shoulder. She subtly shook her head to let him know she didn't agree with her sister. "We ought to stay awhile yet, Anna. Mr. Newcomb's been generous to help out, and I'm wanting you to be stronger before we go off on our own again."

Anna stubbornly asserted, "A change of arrangements will be for the best."

"Whose best?" John folded his arms akimbo and glowered. He'd just been congratulating himself for how happily things had turned out, and now he had to squelch this harebrained plot! At least Emily was being practical. Anna acted as if she didn't have the sense God gave a minnow. "You were starving. Freezing, too. You're both still weak as kittens. Think, Anna—who will care for Timothy while you work?"

"We'll work different hours." She mumbled the words to her lap and still didn't look at him. "I have no proof or papers. Your brother isn't home to confront, and I've decided I don't want to. 'Tis my son, so my voice is all that counts."

"Anna, if you don't want him to see you—"

"I don't want to see him ever again. What if he tries to take my baby?"

"Anna, I'm not concerned about Edward in the least. He's a rascal in some ways, but I cannot fathom he would ever stoop so low as to have done this to you. Truly I think 'tis one of his crew. I'm sure you and Timothy are safe."

Emily gave him a horrified look.

He cleared his throat. "On the obscure chance the babe is my brother's, I'll haul Edward to the altar. He'll wed you properly, Timothy will be legitimate, and I'll keep the *Cormorant* assigned to long voyages if that would make you happy. Instead of troubling ourselves about tomorrow, though, we need to concern ourselves with the present. You sweet women can't possibly make it on your own. Anna, your health is too poor. I can't allow this."

Anna looked up at her sister and whispered in a thready voice, "Emily, we can find work to do at home. Many other women do it. We can, too. Duncan will help. We're a family. We'll pull together."

John pressed. "I won't let anyone take Timmy from you. You cannot let foolish pride come before the welfare of your child."

Anna continued to look up at her sister. Tears streaked down her cheeks. "Please take me back inside."

John swooped to snatch her out of the chair, but she quailed away. He regretted the fact that the truths he spoke went against her wishes. Still, he'd rather be the one to upset Anna than to have her feel Emily was betraying her. He strove to speak to her in his mildest tone. "Anna—"

"No," she whispered in a tearful tone. She stopped even looking up at her sister. Her head drooped as her shoulders shook with sobs. "No."

Emily knelt next to her sister and gathered her in her arms. Anna's weeping tugged at John's heart. He looked helplessly at Emily. She cupped Anna's head to her bosom and rocked her as if she were no more than a tiny lassie. He watched as Emily swallowed hard and blinked back her own tears. Yet, in the midst of the emotional tumult, she still managed to be sure the babe was in no danger of falling out of his mama's lap. *How many problems can this one small woman juggle?*

How many burdens can she carry?

"We'll make it through, our Anna. Aye, we will," Emily promised in a voice thick with tears.

John stood over them and waited a moment. Surely, after the new mother had a few moments, she'd regain her composure. He'd heard women often did considerable crying in the weeks following a birth. He'd give Anna a chance to calm down. With Emily's tender ministrations, he felt certain she'd regain her composure. Minutes stretched. John realized he'd made a grave miscalculation.

Emily looked at him. Her eyes held fathomless sorrow. Deep inside, John felt something shift. At that moment he'd give all he owned to take away the ache in her heart.

In a soft, despairing tone, she said, "It would be best if you left us now, Sir."

John paced away. For a moment he tried to tamp down his emotions. The practical side of him argued with his involvement in this whole mess. He'd done his best by them—providing shelter, warmth, food, and medical care. What more could he do?

Then he glanced back. Every logical excuse sank like an anchor. Anna, tiny little Anna—still thin as could be, so weak she couldn't even walk on her own. She was barely more than a child. She'd been swindled out of her innocence, robbed of the simple joys a young bride usually enjoyed. No matter who fathered her babe, she didn't deserve to endure this.

Even more, he looked at Emily. Originally the woman acted prickly as a curry brush, but they'd worked past that. Day after day she'd welcomed him into the cottage, invited him to share their meals, and listened to his comments about work. He'd never before found a woman who was blind to his windblown hair, calloused hands, and rumpled, end-of-the-workday clothes. He'd given them a dwelling, but she turned it into a home—and warmly opened the door to him. He knew she was grateful, but her reception went beyond that. She didn't look at him and see wealth or power; she saw the sometimes lonely man who split his life between polished society and coarse seamen, and she accepted both aspects without reservation.

He watched as she used that same unconditional love with her sister. Finally Anna calmed down. Emily gave her a gentle squeeze.

Emily normally wore an odd, plain muslin apron that looked like a length of cloth with small ties at the sides and a hole in it for her head. She pulled it off and tied it to form a sash, then carefully tucked the babe in it. John sucked in a sharp breath. He'd never seen the condition of her gown. It was several sizes too big, and even careful stitching couldn't hide the fact that the bodice had been torn badly.

He watched her rise and oh-so-carefully lift Anna upright. One arm held the babe securely as the other wound about Anna's feeble form. Each step they took was an effort. Finally he could bear it no longer. The gravel of the path grated beneath his boots as he strode back to them.

He silently nodded to her, then presumed to stoop and gather Anna into his keeping. He said nothing but took her around the house, across the lawn, up the stairs, and back to her bedchamber. All of her weeping had left little Anna docile and limp. John felt an odd flash of gratitude that in such a state, she wouldn't realize how desperately she'd needed this basic assistance.

John stopped at the bedchamber door for a moment and stared at the bed. The blankets and sheets looked smooth, crisp—folded with military precision so one side lay open to give welcome to a weary woman. Practical, efficient little Emily must have done it when she came in for those few seconds to fetch the babe.

John paced to the bedside. His boots made a ringing noise on the plank floor. Emily followed on his heels. Her silent tread surprised him until he realized she was barefoot. At that realization he wanted to roar. Had he ever seen her wear shoes? He strained to remember, and he seemed to recall a battered pair of boots. Emily continued to wrap the babe in her cut-down blankets, too. He'd been a fool not to consider that they all desperately needed clothing.

Emily paused at the drawer for a moment and settled Timothy in it. She drew a blanket over him, then briskly tugged the hem of Anna's threadbare gown down before whisking the covers over her. John stepped to the side and watched as Emily's rough hand sweetly smoothed back Anna's hair. Softly she crooned, "Sleep now, our Anna."

Anna fell asleep with the speed only a child or an invalid might. Timothy started to fuss, so Emily took him from his makeshift bassinet and carried him into the kitchen. John watched in silence as she managed to warm some milk, add molasses, and slowly spoon it into her nephew. She displayed no awkwardness with the task. Clearly she'd been doing this for days.

"I'll hire a wet nurse."

She looked at him and shook her head adamantly. "No. Anna still has some milk. I'm able to fill in the rest by doing this. 'Twould break Anna's tender heart to know another woman took over suckling her babe, and I cannot do that to her."

"Emily, blame me for not letting you leave. As for the *Cormorant*. . .she'll not return for several months. Anna won't. . ." He cleared his throat.

Grief streaked across her face. She sighed deeply. "She won't have to face him again."

"You will, though."

"That's a bridge I'll cross later. If I catch that rogue, I'm not sure what I'll do."

A wry smile twisted John's mouth. "You're too moral to commit mayhem or murder. If you catch that scoundrel, you'll probably serve him a hefty slice of your mind, then dash straight off to church to pray for his pitch black soul."

She brushed a few errant curls away from her forehead with the back of her wrist. "A blacker soul there never was."

John watched her shift the infant a bit. The prominent seams taken to repair the rip in her clothing no longer lay hidden by the babe's blanketed form. Though he dreaded hearing the answer, John still demanded, "How did your gown get torn?"

" 'Twas torn when I got it."

"I'm not sure whether to be relieved or angry about that."

Emily shrugged. "It doesn't much matter. I'm handy with a needle. Do you know any of the local dressmakers or milliners who might need a worker?"

"If you appear wearing that, they're not going to hire you. What else do you own?"

A bright blush stained her cheeks.

His brows furrowed as he strained to recall the night he'd demanded they pack and come away with him. "Duncan has a change of clothes. Anna's always in her nightdress. I've seen her in two different—" He paused mid-sentence as he realized Emily probably wasn't sleeping in a night rail. She'd given hers to Anna!

Emily turned away and busily twitched an imaginary wrinkle from the corner of Timothy's blanket.

"How many day gowns does Anna own?" Just as surely as he knew his own name, John knew Emily would have the same number or fewer than her sister. He waited grimly for an answer.

"Two." Emily lifted her chin as she answered.

"I trust they're in better condition than the one you're wearing."

Emily's lips thinned into a straight line. She spooned another bit of milk into the babe and gave no reply.

"Answer me."

She continued to feed the babe. Her voice went brittle. "You asked no question."

John pulled out a chair and sat across from her. He leaned forward and rested his forearms on his thighs. Maybe she wouldn't feel so defensive if he didn't tower over her. Certainly, this matter needed to be discussed so he could determine their needs. He should have done so from the start. John waited a moment to let her get accustomed to his nearness, then softened his tone considerably. "Emily, I meant you no offense, and out there—I wasn't trying to be cruel to Anna."

"I know." She shot him a fleeting glance. "You spoke the truth, and as much as it shames me, I'm just as glad you did so I didn't have to." She said nothing more.

John let silence hover and hoped she'd hearken back to their conversation. She didn't. He finally pressed. "I didn't mean to upset you just now, either—asking about your clothing."

She continued to feed the child in silence, carefully drizzling milk from a spoon into little Timothy's tiny pink mouth. Precious little dribbles, patiently given, marked the passage of tense moments. Finally she spoke, but she didn't look at him. "If I'm embarrassed, it's my own fault. This whole mess is my fault."

"How could any of this possibly be your fault?"

"Because I was a fool to allow my sister to be beguiled by that monster. I hold myself to blame. Aye, I do. Edward Newcomb was a handsome man. Too handsome. Smooth his charm was. Silver-tongued, too. I listened to him and fell for his lies as much as Anna did. Never did I suspect he would tell us a pack of lies."

She looked up at him. Her eyes glistened with unshed tears.

"The Edward Newcomb who courted and ruined my Anna isn't so broad across the shoulders as you, and his dark hair defies discipline instead of obeying a comb as does yours, but he shares your strong chin. Then, too, his eyes are the same shade as yours—one I've not seen before or since. 'Tis like the color of tea left to steep fully."

John listened without interrupting. That description lined up too closely with Edward's character and appearance to leave him comfortable.

"He didn't wear clothes so fine as yours." She dipped her head and resumed feeding the babe. Her hand shook as she manipulated the spoon to coax the little one to take more nourishment. "He had quite a few garments, though. Once, when he tore a shirt, he cast it to the corner. We cut it down for Duncan and got a shirt and a few handkerchiefs from it."

John stayed silent. He sensed she wasn't finished speaking yet, but he couldn't understand where the conversation was going. He'd asked about her clothing, not about the rogue who ruined her sister. He bided his time and let Emily control the conversation. Her hands stayed busy, spooning in the milk, wiping the baby's chin.

"Edward made promises. He brought our Anna a ring and produced a man of God—one in vestments who carried a Bible and a missal. Anna's eyes were bright with love light, so I stood there and let her pledge her heart to that rascal. Only then we likened him to one of those princes in a fairy tale. We never suspected the truth.

"Looking back, I know I should have guarded my sister better. 'Twasn't a church wedding, but I overlooked that because we were both wedging the ceremony in the few minutes betwixt our shifts of work.

"Edward told us he had no family—none a'tall. His da perished at sea, and the rest of them died when their house caught fire. He said he'd missed being part of a family. He'd supposedly sold all he had in the whole world to buy the *Cormorant,* so he was living aboard the vessel in the captain's cabin. He said 'twas bad fortune to have a woman aboard a sailing vessel. Because of that, Anna stayed with Duncan and me.

"Edward brought fish for supper often enough. Proud she was of him, our Anna was. Her man could put food on the table. Each time he docked, he brought coal—but only enough to last for the nights when I went to work and Duncan got shoved over to our neighbor's. There never seemed to be sufficient money to buy us wood or coal, but Edward gave Anna a pretty little trinket every now and again.

"He had grand plans, he did. Promised Anna a fine home of her own—one with stairs and a maid and gowns aplenty—all of them beautiful enough for a princess."

Her voice shook as she added, "But he never so much as gave her a dress length of fabric or a bit of yarn so she could knit herself anything at all. He might have put a bit on our table, but he didn't keep a roof over our Anna's head for a single night or put a stitch of clothing on her back.

"He'd be gone for a voyage and return, and she'd be so happy to fall into his arms. We all prayed for each voyage to be successful, for him to be safe, and for the Lord to bless the business so he'd become a good provider for our Anna.

"Fish, we'd eat—and he'd mourn that the voyage hadn't brought him enough profit to do more than pay back a little more of the hefty loan the bank held on the *Cormorant.* Even so, we kept faith in God and in Edward's best efforts."

John sat back in his chair and listened grimly.

Emily drew in a shaky breath. "That last time, I stuck my nose into their marriage. Getting sick most every sunrise, our Anna was, and we were sure of the reason. I got home early in the morning, and Edward sat there, staring at her like she'd told him his boat had run aground. She didn't even have to speak the words. He'd guessed it right quick."

John dreaded what she'd say next, but he held his tongue and let Emily finish the heartbreaking tale. She needed to unburden her heart, if only for a moment.

"Edward didn't seem happy in the least about becoming a father, and Anna cried over his sour attitude. But he told her 'twas only because he'd hoped to have that splendid house for her before they started in on having babes.

"I nosed in then. I told him Anna didn't need a palace; she needed a warm cabin. He needed to stop dreaming up grand schemes for a day far into the future and care for his bride here and now. They could always change up to something better, but in the meantime he needed to start providing for her." Her voice dropped to a chagrined whisper as she confessed, "I told him he'd been having all the pleasures of a husband without assuming the responsibilities."

"You spoke nothing other than the truth, Emily. How long had this been going on?"

"The end of autumn and all of last winter."

"Four months!" John couldn't bear to sit through the tale any longer. He had to hear the rest, but he stood and paced over to the window. He shoved his hands in his pockets and clenched his jaw. He'd been to their shanty—in autumn, not winter—and the cold had been unbearable.

Emily fell silent. He stared at her faint reflection in the window. "You needn't fear me, Emily. I'm not judging you as a shrew at all. I don't know how you tolerated him that long. The circumstances were desperate, and you did what any sensible woman would."

"I'm not so sure of that," she confessed thickly. "Edward brought coal that night and set sail the next day. He'd told Anna earlier that he planned to be home for a whole week. I drove him away with my bitter words."

John wheeled back around. "No, Emily. I won't have you saying such a thing. Your words made no difference—this Edward was a blackguard. The minute a man of his ilk discovers his woman is with child, he decamps. If you'd have never said a thing, he'd still have abandoned her."

"We prayed for him and his ship every day. Aye, we did, and all of us worried the *Cormorant* might have gotten damaged or run aground—or worse. So many months passed without a word."

"And that's common enough, so you waited patiently," he filled in.

Emily nodded. "After he'd been gone a long while and things were getting bad, Anna acted so very brave when she parted with the wee gifts he'd given her. Every last one ended up at the pawnshop. She said 'twas like Edward had given her a way to take care of the babe she carried."

He groaned. Anna's love let her hope and dream that her husband would come back. Emily's guilt made her assume she'd driven the man away. Neither of these innocents understood in all of those months that they'd been deceived, betrayed, and abandoned.

Emily swallowed hard. Her lips quivered as she said, "My sister had nothing left at all, John Newcomb—not a thing but a wedding ring and empty promises. I needed to make every last cent count. 'Twas more important to buy milk and coal than it was for me to have another gown. So you see, I deserve no more than I have."

I deserve no more than I have. Her words echoed in his head. John wanted in the worst way to quiet that aching confession. It kept repeating over and over, haunting him. She'd said she was coming up on nineteen. It sounded older and more responsible that way—but that meant she was eighteen.

She'd been seventeen and Anna was sixteen when a dashing sea captain took unpardonable advantage of their naiveté. Emily shouldn't punish herself for not knowing better.

Ah, but she would. She'd feel responsible; she'd hold herself accountable for anything that tainted the lives and hearts of those she loved. Under her crusty, brave front, she hid a heart too tender to believe. The sacrifices she'd made defied words.

John gently cupped her nape and thumbed delicate spiraling wisps of her beautiful, fiery hair. "Emily, you're worthy of a wardrobe full of fine gowns and a box full of jewels. You cannot punish yourself for what happened. The blackguard had a tainted soul and took sore advantage. Life brings tragedies, and this surely rates among them; but stop faulting yourself and chart a new course in life that will bring some happiness back into your heart."

She set aside the spoon, lifted wee Timothy to her shoulder, and patted his back. Without sparing an upward glance, she whispered, "You ask me to look past today. I cannot. The future holds too much heartache."

"Oh, Em," he said softly. He watched her shudder and gulp back a sob. He tilted her face up to his. "We'll make sure Anna is happy and comfortable."

She compressed her lips and nodded.

"Like you," he said in his quietest tone, lest Anna waken and hear him, "I know how very paltry that notion is. Day or night, you summon me at once if you need anything at all."

ten

John left the cottage and went to his stables. There he motioned to Duncan. The lad dashed to his side at once.

"Aye, Sir?"

"I'd like a word with you." John clasped his hands behind his back and sauntered toward a fence. From the corner of his eye, he watched Duncan copy his posture and shadow his every step. The sight of his blatant imitation forced John to quell a momentary smile. The lad hadn't had a man in his life, so he'd begun to mimic John's moves whenever they spent even a few moments together. It was flattering in a sad, but touching way. John silently vowed to be a good example. He stopped at a fence and stared at a frolicking yearling.

After a moment of silence, Duncan gave him a stricken look. "Did I do something wrong?"

"Nay, not a thing. It occurred to me I ought to know the stable boy I'm trusting with the care of my favorite mounts." John started out what he hoped sounded like a casual conversation. The lad was bright as a copper penny. He loved to chatter. All it took were a few seemingly casual questions, and Duncan gladly volunteered information. After getting him relaxed and assured he was eager to please, John managed to ask, "Did you ever see the courting gifts Edward gave your sister?"

"Oh, I did, Sir! I truly did." Duncan cheerfully shared in great detail the treasures Captain Edward Newcomb had bestowed upon Anna months ago.

With each one the lad described, the gnawing in John's belly grew worse. The physical description Emily gave of Anna's so-called husband, the ring she'd shown, and the gifts Duncan mentioned—they all added up to a picture so appallingly clear that shame scalded him. John patted Duncan on the shoulder. "You're a good little fellow. I know Em and Anna tell you so, but I'm saying, man-to-man, you're a fine buck."

Duncan beamed with pride.

John excused himself, strode home, and looked at his calendar. It confirmed what he'd dreaded: He'd scheduled the *Cormorant* for monthly runs up and down the coast all through the previous autumn and winter. In fact, she'd been in and out at just the right time frame for a quick courtship and the four-month-long sham marriage.

Edward had always been resourceful and fun-loving, but John never once believed he'd stoop to such a level—and he'd blindly defended his brother's honor at the O'Briens' expense.

Grandfather left the entire shipping business to John, but Edward always knew that would be the case. He'd displayed virtually no jealousy five years ago when that plan became a reality. An adventurer by nature, he would never be happy tied down. Indeed, he seemed more than pleased when John made him captain of the *Cormorant*. He'd declared he got the better part of the bargain.

Occasional tales of Edward being indiscriminate with women and wine reached John's ears. Father died just as John was reaching his manhood, so Grandfather took it upon himself to discuss the importance of being morally responsible with women and temperate. John knew Grandfather had the same conversation with Edward, too. After Grandfather died and John suspected Edward hadn't taken that lesson to heart, he'd set aside time and reinforced the wisdom of living an upright life. That brotherly discussion and prayers obviously hadn't been effective.

Since Edward was at sea much of the time, it made no sense for him to keep a home of his own. Instead, John allowed his brother to inhabit the southern wing of the mansion. Rarely did John bother to enter those quarters, but he had every reason to do so today.

The maids cleaned in here on a weekly basis, but the wing was kept locked otherwise. It lay eerily silent now. John didn't know where his brother usually kept everything, but he remembered clearly that the porcelain figurine of a shepherdess customarily stood on the mantel next to a clock. That spot lay empty. The three little gold hearts that once dangled from the key to Edward's generously stocked liquor cabinet no longer hung from the braided scarlet cord. Though John had heard the truth, he needed to see it with his own eyes—and his eyes didn't deceive him as his heart had for the past days. The treasures Anna received from her so-called husband had come from Edward's quarters.

John sank onto a bench by the window. For a flash he dared hope mayhap it wasn't truly Edward. It couldn't be a deckhand, because they didn't have entry to the house. Perhaps one of his employees had stolen his identity and masqueraded as him. Certainly a member of the household staff would have access to the trinkets—but the physical description haunted John. That last burst of hope faded. He knew the bitter, appalling truth.

He trudged out of the house, out to the stables. He quietly ordered a buggy to take him back to Emily's old neighborhood. The driver located the only pawnshop in the area by looking for the three balls hanging from the roof. John somberly ordered the driver to wait. He entered the dingy shop and looked about with a mixture of pity and disgust. Few were the items that counted any value at all. Those who lived in these blocks traded in goods too pathetic to be of value to anyone else. Aching poverty radiated from the sacrifice of a battered flute. Then, too, the better goods clearly hadn't come from this sector of town. The proprietor was savvy enough not to take things that could be traced easily, but some of these goods came from either theft or burglary.

"Ah, Sir!" The shopkeeper toddled up. His red, bulbous nose tattled about a fondness for drink. He quickly took in John's fine clothing, and an avaricious gleam lit his eyes. "Would you be looking for anything special?"

As if reciting loathed Latin declensions, John tonelessly rattled off the list of Anna's treasures Duncan had named.

"Ah, yes. I still have some of those things here. Nice, they are. Quality goods." He bobbed his head, as if to punctuate those words. "Worth a pretty penny, too."

"Get them."

John could scarcely bear to stay in that pawnshop. The proprietor bustled about, then stooped to look in a cabinet. As he straightened up, his lower lip protruded. "My son must've sold the teak candlestick and the ivory fan." He assessed the things he'd managed to locate and named an outlandish price for them.

John looked at the counter and did his best not to snap at the pawnbroker. "Then I'll take those things." He slapped a coin onto the counter, grabbed the other three items Duncan had mentioned, and stalked out.

He'd paid too much, but he had to get out of there. The man was dishonest as a praying snake, and he'd done his best to cheat John. How badly had he bilked valiant little Emily out of a few extra, much-needed pennies?

John looked at the cheap gifts in his lap. He didn't know whether to give them back to Anna or to keep them for when he confronted Edward. What he did know was, as soon as the *Cormorant* docked, Edward was going to have to do some fancy explaining. Even then words would count for naught. John had no idea how best to rectify this sordid mess, but he prayed for wisdom to handle it well.

As he rode back toward the better side of town, he stared at the little porcelain figurine in his hand. Years ago his mother had bought it to use as an example of a costume she wanted to commission for a masquerade ball. Though charming and sentimental, it carried virtually no monetary value. What had it gotten for Anna? An extra quart of milk? He fought the urge to fling it at the street and watch it shatter. The delicate bit of porcelain had been a tool to bribe an innocent. His fingers tightened about the swirling skirts until the edge cut into his hand.

The ground changed from mud to gravel to cobblestone. Aye, he'd left behind the ragged tide of poverty and had reached civilization. Sadly, civilization hadn't done anything to improve Edward's soul. He'd been the beast while the O'Briens, poor as field mice, displayed integrity and honor.

Suddenly something caught John's eye. He called out for the hack to stop, vaulted out, and hastened into a shop.

❧

"Take it. Wear it!" John had waited until the next day to come by. He'd hoped Anna had calmed down and forgiven him. Obviously his hopes were in vain.

He gave Anna an exasperated look. He hadn't anticipated her reaction to his gift. He wanted to shower her with the pretty things that would lift her spirits and fill her last days with the simple joys most women took for granted. Not only that, he knew Emily would take delight in her sister's excitement. But Anna wasn't excited. Why would the silly woman balk at having a simple, ordinary gown when she obviously needed one so desperately?

"Anna, yesterday you were planning to move away and find

employment. If you are that serious about it, at least be sensible enough to admit you'll need suitable attire."

"Yes, Anna," Duncan agreed as he stood by the bedside. The lad tentatively ran his stubby fingers across the day gown's skirt, then pinched the fabric. "He's right, you know. You must wear it. The material is thick as can be! You'll be so warm in it!"

It bothered John that Duncan thought in terms of a garment for warmth.

"It doesn't even need to be mended," Duncan added.

John bit back a growl. When he'd been seven, he would have merely looked at a gown and thought it was a pretty color. The women in his life never suffered cold, hadn't once borne the indignity of having to patch together the tattered remnants of someone else's cast-off clothing, or been faced with relying on charity. They'd never once lifted their soft, lily white hands to do any domestic chore or been forced to fend for anything more than a good seat at a soiree. Emily and Anna had endured far too much of the hard side of life, and Duncan had seen it all.

Duncan stuck out his thumb and poked it down the row of little pewter roses that marched one by one from collar to waist. "Look, our Anna! All the buttons are still on it!"

That did it. John swept the gown out of Duncan's reverent hands and tossed it across Anna's legs. He locked gazes with her, then gave her a boyish grin and wagged his finger emphatically. "I don't know what to do with you, Anna. You're supposed to help me here. If you won't put on your new gown, Emily won't, either. Don't you want her to wear hers?"

"Yes," Anna confessed with a sigh.

"Much better," he teased. He didn't want to bully her, so he hoped this change of tactics was in the right vein. "As soon as I leave, you can put it on. By three I expect Emily to be wearing hers, too. She ought to be home by then."

"Of course she will," Anna agreed.

John nodded. He knew she'd not jeopardize Anna's health by being gone long at all. She often found a quiet place to pray, so when he saw her Bible wasn't on the table and her shawl wasn't on its customary hook, he presumed she'd stolen away for devotions.

"What's happening at three?" Duncan asked.

"We're going for a ride in my buggy. Don't you think that would be a fun outing?"

"Oh, yes, Sir!"

"After the outing, we'll drop you off at the stables while your sisters and I have a talk. You'll get your new suit of clothes later because I've arranged for Mr. Peebles to give you a riding lesson."

John left with the sounds of Duncan's excited whoops still ringing in his ears. He arrived back at the caretaker's cottage at three o'clock sharp. He consulted with his gold pocket watch to confirm the time, snapped it shut, and headed up the walk. He knew Anna would look nice in her new gown, but he especially wanted to see Emily. He'd chosen a fine, fawn-colored merino wool for her, one with a small vine pattern the exact same green as her pretty eyes. Instead of relying on an excess of lace and ribbons, the beauty of the dress lay in its simplicity—just as Emily's loveliness lay in her queenly posture and warm spirit. The moment he spied it, he'd known the gown would look stunning on her.

The carriage rolled up the drive as he mounted the steps. *Indeed,* he said to himself, *this will work out well enough. The women have had sufficient time to fuss and get ready.*

He planned to collect the O'Briens and take them on a simple outing. Anna couldn't stay out of bed for very long, but he'd spoiled her little picnic yesterday. He craftily planned this so he'd entice Emily on a trip.

What could be better than a stop at the mercantile to let Emily and Anna choose some slippers and yardage? He'd be catching two fish with one worm that way. At least once in her short life, Anna would enjoy shopping for pretties and gew-gaws, and Emily would get clothing she so desperately needed.

Women tended to prefer certain colors over others, so since he had no notion as to what they needed, he'd do well to let the O'Brien women look over the bolts and make their own selections. While they did that, he'd have a clerk help him fit Duncan with some breeches and shirts.

As for the baby, John couldn't begin to decide what Timothy required. Blankets, little gowns, and diapers he knew about—whatever else an infant required, he didn't know. Judging from the fact that Emily seemed to do a constant round from wash bucket to clothesline, he assumed she'd know best. But he'd bought twenty-five yards of white cotton on the advice of his laundress, Gracie. Aye, Emily was so clever that she'd make the tiny garments and cut out nappies.

John had arrived at some conclusions. After they returned to the little cottage, he'd sit Emily down and set her straight on matters. As for Anna, he'd gently let her know he was her ally and fully believed it was his brother who had dishonored her. He'd apologize both for his own stubbornness and for the pain Edward had caused her.

His brother was responsible for this mess. Not a shred of doubt remained in John's mind. He'd spent all last night anguishing over the fact that he'd been so busy with business, he hadn't been a good brother. He'd thought he knew his brother well, when in all actuality, he didn't. Family allegiance had blinded him, and even when proof mounted, John foolishly allowed himself to hope this was just a sad case of stolen or mistaken identity. In spite of his stubborn ignorance, the facts finally culminated in his accepting the galling truth. Honor demanded he start to right the wrongs as best he could. Several remedies existed—none of them seemed good, though.

At any rate, the O'Briens were ethically and morally—if not legally—family now. Determined to fulfill duty in his profligate brother's stead and salvage the family name to some degree, John forged ahead. He'd resolutely determined to put a fresh face on matters as of this noon.

The front door of the little cottage stood open, and Duncan stayed busy, sweeping the floor. John frowned. "Put down the broom and wash up a bit, Lad. Where are your sisters? I was very specific that you were all to be ready to leave promptly at three."

Duncan propped the broom in the corner. "No, Sir, they're not ready."

"I'm not in a mood to put up with two stubborn women digging in their heels and pitching a fit," he told the boy.

Duncan looked at him somberly. He reached for the broomstick and hugged it to his scrawny chest. "I don't think Anna's up to pitching much of anything, Sir. Something's wrong with her."

"Emily?" John strode to the bedchamber door and knocked once. Emily didn't respond, and his concern mounted. "Emily!" He rapped harder, then gave up on proprieties and let himself in.

Emily didn't even turn to face him. She leaned over Anna and blotted her face with a wet cloth. In a strained voice, she said, "Oh, John—she just collapsed. Please fetch the doctor!"

eleven

No one answered his knock, so John figured Emily likely had both hands full with the baby. He pushed aside the black crape ribbon, opened the latch, and stepped over the threshold. Though prepared to call out a muted greeting, the words died on his lips.

Emily sat on the settee. Duncan lay there, huddled into a sad little ball, resting his head in her lap. She held Anna's child to her shoulder and dully looked up at John. Grief rode her hard, robbed her eyes of their pretty sparkle, and left her cheeks gray.

"Emily," John said softly as he crossed the floor. He fought the urge to pull her into his arms. "Cook mentioned you sent for me."

"Oh." It took her a moment before she remembered why she'd wanted to see him. "I wanted to thank you."

He didn't reply. The funeral had been private. He and the vicar agreed to bury Anna in consecrated ground. She'd been laid to rest in the warm woolen gown he'd bought her, and he'd added a small, gold cross about her throat. After Emily silently slipped the ruby-chip "wedding ring" onto her sister's lifeless finger, she turned away. John led her into the kitchen, clasped her to his chest, and held her as her sobs drowned out the sound of their closing the casket. The burial service was simple, small, and quiet—just as Anna had been.

Now the babe fussed. Emily shifted him automatically. She looked down at her brother and back to John. "Would you still be willing to let Duncan have that job you offered?"

"Duncan does a fine job with my horse."

Her brows puckered slowly, as if something troubled and confused her; then she shook her head. "No, I meant the other one you mentioned when we were living at our own place. Duncan would work hard for you and could earn a wee bit. I trust you to be fair about his wages. I spoke with Madam Victorine, and she'll allow me to stitch for her at home, so I can keep watch over little Timothy. If you—"

"Emily!" John stared at her in disbelief. "What are you thinking?"

She looked at him almost blankly. "We have to—" She paused and moistened her lips, then tried again. "It will work. I found a room—"

"No!" He wheeled about, stepped off three paces, then turned back again. He couldn't let them go. The cottage usually lay vacant—it didn't inconvenience him to allow her to occupy it. Even if it did cause him a few logistical problems, he'd move heaven and earth to keep her here. At least then he'd know she was safe, warm, and fed. He locked gazes with her. "You're not going anywhere."

"I'll never forget your kindness to A–Anna."

"I did nothing for her!"

Emily stared at him. Her eyes held an ache he could barely stand to see. His voice sounded rough as he asserted, "You don't need to make any decisions right now. Stay here—at least for a few months."

Emily shook her head. "You've been more than generous. Even if Edward lied, you showed great personal honor to provide grandly for our Anna. He duped us, but that's all in the past now. Duncan and I never expected Anna's husband to take us on. I have to face the fact that a man who wouldn't even claim his own wife won't have anything to do with her relatives. He'll certainly never want a thing to do with a child he sired on the wrong side of a blanket."

"Don't you even think—"

"Oh, I've thought long and hard, Mr. Newcomb. My mind is set. I refuse to be a burden, weighing you down. We're not your responsibility."

"What if I want you to be my responsibility?"

"My brother and I will care for our own."

"You can't take care of yourselves, let alone a babe!" He scowled. "Besides, Timothy isn't just your nephew; he's my nephew, too!"

Emily's eyes shot fire. She gave her brother's arm a little squeeze. "Go check the nappies on the line to see if they're dry yet."

Duncan picked up on his sister's surge of emotions and hastened out the door. Emily watched him leave, then turned back to John. Her arms tightened around the babe. "You said the marriage wasn't valid. You never once recognized Anna"—her voice cracked as she said her sister's name—"never acknowledged her as Edward's wife. You have no reason or right to step in now and claim this babe."

"I was wrong."

"Well, you can just stay wrong! Don't you even think about calling Timmy your nephew!"

"We both know he is."

"You have no proof," she stated implacably, turning the tables on him.

John stared at her and tried to conquer his impatience.

Emily stared right back at him. Something in his eyes frightened her. All night she'd thought matters through. It was for the best that she move now. His reaction only proved it. She repeated herself. "No, you have no proof at all."

"Your Bible has the marriage listed!"

Emily cranked her head to the side and choked back a sob.

How could he, of all people, bring that up now? "You yourself said anything could be written in a Bible."

John quietly closed the distance between them. He sat beside her on the settee. His closeness disturbed her, but she stayed still. Part of her wanted to leap up and dash away from him; a greater part of her wanted to lean into him and borrow his strength and consolation. She couldn't allow herself such weakness—especially now when he was suddenly changing his tune and making claims on Anna's wee babe.

John cradled her chin with a calloused hand and turned her face to his. "I know what I said, and I regret every word of it. You're old enough to understand people sometimes say things they don't mean."

"Oh, yes. I've learned that." Her laugh sounded bitter, even to her own ears. She moved away from his touch. "Whoever he was, that scoundrel told lies aplenty and pledged a false marriage vow with his hand on that very Bible. I don't need you to tell me men say things they never intend to honor."

"You're ripe for the plucking, Emily, and there are many men out there who would take advantage of you. Stay here. Let me provide for—"

"Your offer is generous, but I'll not be a kept woman."

Impatience tinged his tone. "I had no scurrilous intentions! All I wanted was to make sure you could care well for my nephew."

Her heart clenched, and she bolted to her feet. "Anna went to her grave, shamed to the core of her soul. How could you even think to speak these words now? A week ago they would have helped. She admired you, and had you but even hinted you believed 'twas your own brother's child—" Words failed her. Emily took a few deep breaths to try to tamp down the violent storm of emotions raging in her breast.

His brows furrowed. "Emily—"

"It's too late now. It's much too late for you to change your mind." Unable to contain herself any longer, she darted to the bedchamber and shut the door behind her.

૨૦

John could hear her weeping. He paced back and forth a few times, unsure of what to say or do. Every single word out of her mouth had been true. Worse—she'd not flung them at him in spite. She'd said them out of the brokenness of her grief.

The whole while she'd clutched the babe as if he were ready to snatch him away. Didn't she understand he wouldn't cause her any further sorrow? Any fool who spent five minutes with her would plainly see her bottomless devotion to the babe. The way her face softened, the color of her eyes deepened, and her small body curled lovingly around little Timothy sang eloquently of how she cherished him. Clearly, to take the child from Emily's keeping would shatter her.

John's only motive was to make things easier for her, to ease her lot in life, and make it possible for her to continue to mother her little nephew and Duncan without having to work herself into utter exhaustion. An inner voice whispered, *But how was she to know my reasons and plans?*

John looked about the tiny cottage. She'd considered it such a splendid home. She'd scrubbed and bustled and filled it with sunshine and laughter. For a few days, these plain walls weren't big enough to hold in all the love in Emily's world; now they weren't strong enough to contain the grief in her anguished heart.

Her crying continued. Every moment he'd fought the urge to go comfort her, but John feared he'd only make it worse.

twelve

Shuffling footsteps made John turn around.

Duncan held a stack of nappies against his chest. "These are dry now." Once he heard his sister's weeping, his already lackluster face clouded over.

"Would you like me to take those to her?" John asked quietly.

Duncan's lower lip quivered. He stared straight ahead as he blinked. "I'm 'posed to be strong 'cuz I'm the man of the family." His small shoulders lifted and dropped from a big sigh; then he turned a bit and gave John a defeated look.

John closed the distance between them, set aside the nappies, and pressed Duncan snug against his leg. "How about if I be the man, and you'll be my assistant? We'll make fine partners."

"We will?"

"Aye," he said, using his most definite tone. "We want good things for your sister, don't we?"

Duncan somberly nodded and blinked back tears.

"Emily is a special woman—a very special woman. She deserves the best we can do for her." He jostled Duncan gently and gave him a man-to-man look. "I need your help. I'll see to Emily, and you take care of Timmy. Can you do that?"

"Yes, Sir."

The boy's bravery pulled at John's heart. He'd never spent time with children other than the occasional cabin boys aboard ship. They all counted a few more years to their short lives than this lad. Grief stricken as he was, he'd not misbehaved a bit. He'd followed Emily's example and tried to see to obligations far too heavy for him to shoulder.

John led Duncan to the doorway and let him open it. His heart lurched. She knelt beside the bed, her face buried in the blankets on what had been Anna's side. Her shoulders shuddered with her sobs; yet the baby lay securely in the bend of one of her arms up on the mattress. Her other hand clenched the blankets.

Just standing in the room brought back the sad memory from a few days ago when Emily had held Duncan tight to her side and whispered one last desperate prayer. Dr. Quisinby had looked over their bowed heads at John and subtly shook his head.

Sweet Emily had borne too much, and John knew he'd foolishly spoken the truth far too late and caused her more heartache. Quietly he knelt beside her and called her name. He picked up her hand and rubbed it. For an instant her fingers curled around his. He closed his hand around hers before she could reclaim it. Her hand fit in his perfectly—small enough to be fully protected, yet capable enough to partner him in whatever they eventually decided to do with the baby.

Slowly her head turned, and her lashes lifted just a bit. He couldn't be sure she'd even seen him through the tears.

Bless his little heart—Duncan went to her other side and cuddled close. "Are you praying, our Em?"

John stretched his other arm across and tucked them both into his embrace. "Prayer is always a good idea." He bowed his head and gave Emily's hand a light squeeze. "Heavenly Father, we've come to kneel at Your feet in the time of our greatest sorrow." As he continued to pray, Emily's crying tapered off, and she curled her fingers back around his hand.

When he finished praying, John patted Duncan's back. "Tuck the little fellow under your arm and carry him off to the main room. Most likely he needs one of those nappies you just brought in."

"Yes, Sir. What are you going to do?"

John gently smoothed his hand over Emily's hair. "I'd like to talk to your sister."

Emily let out a choppy sigh and started to rise.

John sprang to his feet and helped her up. He kept hold of her elbow and led her back out to the settee.

Emily barely waited until he sat down. She wove her fingers together and whispered, "I flung words at you in anger, John Newcomb. I'm giving you my apology, but that doesn't mean I'm letting you get your hands on the babe."

"It was never my intent to take Timothy from you. You have my word—I'll never take him from you. That being said, I've earned your anger, Emily. So much of this is my fault. All this time I believed I knew Edward. I was so sure, but I was wrong. I grew so busy with work that I failed to take time as I should have to be my brother's keeper."

"No, John. I'll not have you blame yourself for the wrongs he did. They were his doing and his alone."

"But, Emily, even so—I should have known him well enough to suspect he was capable of this. Think of how close you are to Duncan. You'd know in an instant if he were up to mischief."

She gave him a sad smile. "But Edward fooled me just as much as he did you, John. You told me to stop punishing myself. I'm thinking you ought to pay heed to your own advice."

He reached over and gently twirled a few of her wispy curls around his finger. Delicate, yet strong. . .feminine, but fiery. He shook his head. "Dear little Em, what are we going to do?"

"You just prayed for God to lead us. I'm not overly good at waiting, but I'm supposing that's what's next."

He chuckled and drew her head to his shoulder. To his

satisfaction, she rested her cheek there as if she belonged nowhere else in the world. For a spell he simply sat and cradled her in his arms. This moment of peace betwixt them felt right. Aye, it did, and that bore some reflection—but later. For now he'd simply relish these few minutes when she finally found respite from her sadness in his arms.

She stirred a bit, but he tenderly murmured, "Shh, Sweetling. Rest."

A short while later, Duncan tiptoed up. "We did good, Mr. John. We are good partners! Look—you got Sis to sleep, and I have Timmy dry as a brick in an oven."

"Nicely done," John praised him under his breath. He wondered if Emily would stay calm if he carried her to bed. In the past she'd startled awake so violently. Then again he just needed to shift her a bit and slip an arm behind her legs. "Em, everything's right as rain. You just keep dreaming," he murmured softly as he lifted her into his arms and rose. The reassurances worked. She didn't so much as wince.

After he tucked her in and shut the door, he went in search of Duncan. The lad was hunkered into a small heap on his cot near the kitchen. The babe lay bundled in Emily's old cutdown blankets in his lap. Duncan awkwardly tried to coax a spoonful of fluid into the infant. He looked up at John and wrinkled his nose. "Our Em is better at this than I am."

John sat down next to him and scowled at the way the babe let out a noisy howl. "I'll hire a wet nurse."

"Em won't like that. She loves babies and wants to care for him, herself."

The baby let out another wail. John tentatively reached out and took him. He'd never held the babe. In fact, he realized, as he fumbled to hold little Timothy, that he'd never once in all his years held a single babe. Emily made it look so easy. He remembered how she carefully supported the head, so he curled his long fingers to cup the little fellow's skull. A shift here, an adjustment there—an awkward moment, then Timothy let out a bellow to make it clear he wasn't happy in the least.

"Eh, now. He's got his toes stuck in your watch fob," Duncan observed.

"Oh." John remedied that minor problem and murmured, "There. That ought to suit you, Man-child."

Timothy wailed more.

John frowned. He cast a quick glance back toward Emily's door. Common sense said he needed her to come rescue him from his incompetence; pride made him want to master this minor debacle—both to prove to himself he was equal to the task and to allow Emily to nap.

Half an hour later, John sat on the cot in his shirtsleeves. He'd shed his suit coat quickly enough. Next, the slate blue silk vest joined the coat on the table since the baby's little toes kept getting tangled in the fob. He'd dropped the cloth Duncan used to mop Timothy's messy face, so he untied his crisp, white cravat and used it to dab at the streak of milk slipping from the babe's little mouth into his neck creases. That concoction of milk and goodness-only-knew-what-else smelled sweet enough, but Timothy had a knack for spitting out as much as he swallowed. The sleeve of John's shirt had an ever-increasing damp spot from all Timothy managed to eject. *No wonder Emily is so tired. She's waking up at night and going through this ordeal.*

Duncan watched in utter silence.

John glanced up at the lad, then nudged Timothy's lower lip with the spoon. "What are you thinking, Duncan?"

"It's a good thing you run a business better than you tend a babe, else you'd be a pauper, Sir."

John chuckled at that assertion. "I can't deny a word you said."

"Em is good with Timothy. Tender and careful."

Something in the lad's tone made John study his somber little features carefully. "Duncan, have I ever said a word about taking Timothy away from you and Emily?"

"No, Sir." The boy then blurted out, "You can't! He's ours. Em said Edward is a scoundrel. She's Timmy's aunt—almost his mother, you know—and I'm his uncle. She said we've got to go 'cause if Edward ever takes Baby Timothy, he'll turn our wee babe into a bad rascal. It's our place to rear him right and to teach him about God. I don't think Edward knows God, because he's a bad man."

John paused. Timothy let out an indignant squawk, so he quickly spooned in another dribble of milk. Duncan's explanation shed considerable light on why Emily wanted to move immediately. It nearly broke John's heart to see how she'd willingly live in a dingy one-room habitation, suffer cold and hunger—all for the sake of her nephew's soul. He'd need to do something—but what?

Timothy let out a pitiful sound.

"That does it." John stood.

Duncan scrambled to his feet. "What are you doing?"

"I'm going to get this babe fed."

Duncan scrambled along beside him. "Pardon me, Sir, but you weren't doing such a fancy job of it."

John inexpertly held the babe over his shoulder. A second later, the babe rewarded that action with a sticky wet spot on his collar.

"You forgot the burp cloth." Duncan grabbed John's pant leg and tried to tug him to a stop by the front door. "Sir, I thought you were just going to walk him to calm him. You cannot take our baby away. Please don't do that. He's all we have."

"We're just going to get him fed and bring him back. You're coming along, so you can stop fretting."

John flipped a blanket over the babe, strode toward his home, and silently prayed that one of the women in the flock of cooks, maids, gardeners' wives—someone, anyone among the lot of them—was suckling a babe and had milk to spare.

Late afternoon sun slanted through the windows. *Whatever am I doing, napping the day away?* Emily shoved off the blankets and got up. Someone tapped on the door. "Yes?"

"Supper's ready, Sis."

Emily smoothed her hair and clothes, then went out to the main room. John and Duncan both stood by the table. She felt her cheeks grow warm. "Pardon me for being a sluggard."

"The notion of you being a sluggard," John said, "is almost as ridiculous as me setting sail across the Atlantic in a wash basin."

Emily's smile faded abruptly when she saw the table. Three place settings awaited them. John came to dinner only when she invited him, and she hadn't done so now. The third place Duncan must have set out of habit—or his youthful hope that Anna would "come back." Her heart leapt to her throat.

"I have an evening appointment so we'll need to talk while we dine."

As soon as he finished the prayer, Emily looked around. "Where is Timothy? He must be starving by now."

"Oh, you needn't worry, Em." Duncan smiled. "Mr. Newcomb made sure he got fed."

Feeding Timothy was no easy feat. Emily looked at their guest in amazement. In her wildest imaginings, she couldn't fathom how this huge man managed to hold a small feeding spoon in his great hands—let alone deliver it to a squirming, noisy infant. "You fed the baby?"

"I tried," he confessed.

"He's terrible at it," Duncan declared.

John took a sip of coffee. "I met with little success so I asked my laundress to feed him. He's on a blanket behind the settee, if you want to be sure I brought him back."

Emily stared at John and shook her head. "I don't need to. You gave me your word you'd not take Timothy away from me. You're an honorable man, and you've never once lied to me."

The warmth of John's smile made her heart beat a bit faster. He tilted his head toward her plate. "Eat. You're going to need your energy if you accept my plan."

"What plan?"

He blotted his mouth with a napkin, then smiled at her. "I'm sure you've noticed my cook is very accomplished."

She nodded.

He chose his words carefully in deference to the delicacy of the topic. "She is to be blessed with a child in the next month or so. My laundress already has a seven-month-old son. As I mentioned, she saw to young Timothy's hunger today."

Emily blinked at him, unable to comprehend why he would tell her these things.

"The laundress's mother, who's been watching the baby, is in poor health. My head gardener's youngest daughter, Mary, is twelve. I thought perhaps she could come stay with you during the daytime, and betwixt the two of you, you could tend Timothy and the other babies."

"Mr. Newcomb—"

"Oh, Em, you love babies so!" Duncan wiggled excitedly in his seat.

"And Gracie—the laundress—will wet-nurse Timothy each morning and evening when she drops off and picks up her little one. She can come at noon to feed him, too. Her own babe is eating some table food, so she has an abundance and doesn't mind sharing. When Cook has her babe, she'll come by, and she said she'll feed Timothy as well."

Emily moistened her lips. "I'm to sit at home and rock

Timothy whilst this young Mary tends Gracie's boy? We won't even have the cook's babe for another month. Mr. Newcomb, you're trying to dress charity in a comely costume, but 'tis charity, nonetheless."

He shook his head and flashed her a smile. "It's not charity at all. You'd be performing a valuable service for me. This way I can keep my staff." He looked at his plate meaningfully. "I don't want to think of losing my cook!"

Duncan and John carried on the conversation and quickly changed the topic. Emily felt they'd boxed her right into their tidy little scheme. The odd thing was, it didn't bother her. If anything, she felt relieved. She'd still be able to provide for Duncan and Timothy.

Lord, I give You my thanks. It's been so verra hard, but You've carried me through this far. I'm grateful. You've put John Newcomb in our lives—not just for the creaturely comforts he's given, but for how he's become a fine example to Duncan. Bless this man, Father, for how he's gone out of his way to help us. Amen.

"Emily!" Duncan tugged on her sleeve.

"Huh?" She suddenly realized their conversation had waned during the moments she prayed and considered the new venture John proposed.

John gave her a strained look. He reached over and wiped a tear from her cheek.

She wrinkled her nose and gave him a watery laugh. "I'm being silly. I was thinking on how much easier 'twill be to care for three babes than all of the people at Wilken's Asylum—and I'll have a helper!"

John shook his head. "A woman must be God's biggest mystery. She cries when she's pleased."

❧

"Crocuses!" Emily stared at the damp flowers in John's large hands.

He stamped slush off his boots, then came inside. "Aye. The promise of spring." He carefully handed them to her and looked her in the eye and said in a gentle murmur, "A reminder that there is new life through the Resurrection and God's hand tends everything, even through the darkest months."

"Oh, John, thank you. I needed to be reminded of that." Emily held the flowers and realized he'd brushed away the snow to cut them. That fact touched her heart even more. He'd been a godsend. On the days she grieved the deepest, John had a knack for saying something that brought comfort. Truly the Lord used him to remind her of His present and future solace.

John peeled out of his greatcoat and hung it on a brass hook by the door. "The new ship is to be delivered on the morrow."

"How big is it?" Duncan asked.

"A schooner. Three-masted. Same plans and size as the *Gallant*."

Duncan jigged from one foot to the other. "Can I see her?"

"Now, Duncan, Mr. John is a busy man." Emily gave her brother a stern look.

"We'll all go see her on Sunday after church," John declared. "I'm eager to show her off."

Emily poured water into her extra teapot and arranged the crocuses in it. She fussed as she set them on the table. No one had ever given her flowers. The gesture wasn't a romantic one, and she didn't mistake it as such, but the thoughtfulness of the act and the comforting words that accompanied them warmed her to the depths of her soul.

A knock sounded, and the door swung open without anyone answering it. Gracie and Cook both traipsed straight in. "Hello! How are the babies?"

"Fat and sassy," Emily said. "Gracie, that son of yours is starting to crawl."

Gracie and Cook bustled over to the table and set their

baskets on it. By now they had the routine down. They'd deliver supper as they picked up their little ones. Often as not, John would instruct Cook to deliver his supper, too, so he could sup with them in the cottage instead of at his own table. Though it baffled Emily that he would do so, his presence always resulted in a lively discussion over the meal.

While Cook claimed Timothy and nursed him in the bed-chamber, Emily and Gracie set the table. The laundress then took her wee one and left for home. "See you in the morning!"

With Cook still in the house and Duncan underfoot, Emily didn't fret about John's spending time there. No one could gossip about anything that innocent and open. She lifted little Violet from the cradle and carried her over to the table. The routine worked flawlessly. When Timothy finished nursing, Cook would come out, place him in the cradle, take Violet, and go back to John's big house. Since Cook was tending Timothy now, Emily sat down, and John asked a blessing on the meal.

"Family tradition is to wait to name a vessel until it is delivered," John said as he cut his roast. "I thought we could talk over some possibilities."

"What about the *Sea Tiger*?" Duncan suggested.

"That sounds exciting, but it won't work." John set down his knife. "My grandfather always named his vessels after birds—the *Cormorant,* the *Osprey,* and the *Peregrine.*"

"Why did that stop?" Emily wondered.

"My father was a staunch abolitionist. He commissioned and got only one vessel before he died: the *Freedom.* When Grandfather started handing the reins of the business over to me, he told me to devise my own theme. I settled on using character traits."

"The *Resolute,* the *Gallant,* the *Allegiant,*" Emily thought aloud. From their discussions, she knew much about John's business.

"Aye. So now I'm faced with trying to come up with something suitable."

"Loyalty. Honesty," Duncan suggested as he tore open a roll and slathered butter on it.

"Kindness sounds too. . .weak," Emily mused. She looked at John and knew kindness was an underrated force that had the power to change things. He embodied so many fine qualities. Surely another of his traits would make for a grand name for his new vessel. "Something stronger, perhaps. Stalwart. Courageous."

"Those have possibilities." John took a gulp of coffee. "Victorious. Persistence."

They continued to toss around names clear through dessert. By the time John took his leave, he'd narrowed his choices down to either the *Reliant* or the *Stalwart*.

Later, after she'd tucked both Timothy and Duncan in for the night, Emily fingered the crocuses and whispered, "Lord, thank You for this reminder of eternal life. Bless John Newcomb in a special way, Father, for his constancy and consolation. Between him at my table and You in my heart, I don't feel so alone."

❧

Three months later, John received a message from the captain of a frigate. Edward sent word that the *Cormorant* had limped into port in Georgia after a storm. Many of the sails were shredded, and a portion of the starboard bulkhead suffered appreciable damage when the mainmast snapped. Six other vessels also sustained severe damage and required attention, so Edward estimated it would be another six weeks before all of the *Cormorant*'s repairs were effected and she'd be ready to return to Virginia.

Part of John itched for Edward to come home so he could settle the matters at hand. The other part of him got caught in an undertow of relief. He'd been praying for wisdom, but he didn't yet know how to handle this.

In the meantime, he stopped by to see how Emily fared. No stranger to grief, she continued to accomplish whatever needed to be done. Even with the ache evident in her eyes, he saw her smile.

"Duncan carried heavy responsibilities and worries, but I'm thinking he needs a chance to be a carefree boy," she confided in John one afternoon. "I can sit and mope through each day, but then where does that put us? He's so very excited at how you've got him sitting up on a pony. Oh, and those books you brought? He's working hard at them. I'm hoping maybe I can talk to the teacher and find out what a boy his age ought to be learning."

"Emily, I've been meaning to talk to you about that. It was important for the two of you to comfort one another, so I didn't push to have him go, but I think it's time for Duncan to attend school."

"It's too far away, and it's much too late in the year."

John tilted her face up to his. "He can ride along with the other stable boys and the maid's little sister. They go each morning, and it'll be nice for him to get a taste for going to school."

"He'll be so excited. I've done my best to give him lessons, but it's nothing like having a real teacher. Just as he was getting old enough for book learning, Anna got sick and needed his help. We could only dream of him being lucky enough to go to school. You're making another of our dreams come true, John."

John chuckled. "That's really nothing on my part, Emily. The school welcomes all the local children."

The next day was a Saturday. John arrived with a slate, a fancy blue leather book strap, three schoolbooks, and a tin lunch bucket. "Come Monday morning, the wagon will stop right out on the drive for you, Duncan."

"Oh, Em! Can I go? Truly can I?"

Her laughter made the trip John had taken to the school and mercantile more than worth it. He loved her laughter. She didn't laugh nearly often enough—and he planned to change that fact.

"Well, now, the bucket isn't empty, Em!"

"It isn't?" She leaned forward to look inside.

Duncan clutched the bucket and giggled. "Cookies, Em! John brought cookies!"

❧

Emily bit off the thread and threaded her needle. She'd stitched a shirt for Duncan, and from the scraps of cotton left, she'd cut out several handkerchiefs for John. With great care, she hemmed the squares, then chose dark brown thread—the exact color of his eyes—to monogram his initials on them. It wasn't much, but she wanted to do something to show her appreciation to him.

He'd often either have tea or a meal with her and Duncan. She came to look forward to his stories about his workdays and the events in town. He gave Duncan a small knife and was teaching him to whittle, and he'd been present for their celebration for Timothy's first tooth. He loaned Emily books, and they would discuss them. Their conversations about literature and the Bible gave her glimpses of his intellect, wit, humor, and character. The more she came to know him, the more intriguing he became.

Oh, John kept claiming she earned her keep, but she knew better. He had the gift of generosity. God had blessed him, and instead of hoarding his wealth, he turned around and showed kindness to everyone who worked for him. Aye, he was a man to admire—strong, kind, gentle. Emily told herself everyone felt that way about him, but in her heart she knew her feelings ran dangerously deep.

thirteen

John sat at the enormous oak desk in his office and looked out the window for the twentieth time that morning. After last night's summer squall, everything looked clean and slick. From his vantage point, he could see the entire dock.

He'd heard from a ship that just came in that the *Cormorant* was right behind it and should dock either today or tomorrow. John felt grateful for that news. It had been almost seven months since she'd been in port. Though he'd been praying about what to do, he still felt no sense of direction as to how he should handle Edward. Every time he considered how his brother had taken advantage of the O'Briens, his temper soared. The predicament was, if he unleashed his anger, he'd likely create more problems than he solved.

Late in the afternoon, John slammed a ledger book closed. He'd accomplished precious little today. If the *Cormorant* hadn't arrived by now, she wouldn't make it 'til tomorrow. No use waiting around here. He bade Franklin a good evening and left.

On his way home, John checked on the O'Briens. Judging from the line full of sun-dried nappies and snowy little gowns, Gracie must have been by earlier. She and Emily enjoyed doing the babies' laundry together. He felt glad Em had a woman friend to chat with.

He pulled a dozen of the cotton rectangles from the line and chuckled. A year ago he'd not known what shape of cloth a nappy was, let alone how to change one. Having Em, Duncan, and Timothy around domesticated him—and it was an improvement. Newcomb Shipping thrived, even with him there less. He'd started to look at the world around him instead of focusing solely on logs and ledgers.

The gravel crunched beneath his boots as he toted an armful of nappies to the door. He loved coming to the caretaker's cottage. Somehow, in the last month or so, it came to feel like his own home. He regularly took his meals here, and Emily's presence at the humble table in this sunny kitchen was what made all the difference.

Duncan scampered down the five little porch steps just as John reached the door. The lad grinned and shoved the last bite of a bun in his already-full mouth and raced off to the stables. Emily didn't realize Duncan had left a caller at the door, so John stepped in, nudged the door shut, leaned against the sill, and took stock of her.

Over the past months, she'd eaten well and filled out so she glowed with good health. The green dress she'd made for herself brought out the color of her eyes. Late afternoon sun slanted through the window, giving her hair a burnished gleam. She radiated warmth and beauty.

She was reading her Bible and using her toes to tilt the runners on the cradle to keep Cook's daughter rocking contentedly. Gracie's babe lay on a blanket on the floor, an ivory teething ring he must have been gnawing on abandoned as he napped. Timothy lay beside him, his thumb in his mouth. So far, having Emily play nanny to the babes seemed to be working out beautifully.

At times Emily couldn't hide her grief. But right this instant she was the picture of serenity. He'd purchased the cloth for her dress, knowing full well society dictated she ought to be wearing crow black for mourning. Instead he'd chosen an unembellished cotton and hoped its plainness and her manners would keep her from fretting over the pretty, deep green color. In a move to acknowledge her mourning and quiet any qualms, John provided a black kerseymere shawl for her to drape over her shoulders. Emily deserved nice things in her life—she'd suffered long enough.

The day he'd arrived with that shawl, she'd had a small package wrapped in brown paper for him. How she managed to be so shy at times, then so fiery at others, never ceased to amuse him. She'd blushed and quietly handed him the package.

"Oh, look at this!" he exclaimed as he caught sight of the handkerchiefs. "Em, these are—"

"Little nothings," she demurred.

He lifted her face to his. "Emily, I don't ever recall anyone giving me a gift just because their heart told them to. I've been given birthday and Christmas gifts, but those were times when others traditionally make an effort. You—you did this, and I can't figure out how you made the time to do them." He folded one and tucked it into his pocket then and there. "But I'm thankful you did."

He always kept one of them in his pocket. She'd made enough for him to have one a day for a whole week. He stuffed his hand in his pocket now and wadded it up as he struggled again for the millionth time to decide what to do once his brother docked.

On his way home, John had decided to inform her of Edward's impending arrival. The caretaker's cottage sat next to the drive leading to the main house. It would be unfair to leave Emily unprepared for the sight of him. John had yet to discuss Edward with Emily and seek her opinion. Strong willed as she was, he suspected she'd decided on a course of action.

"Oh!" Emily's pretty green eyes went huge when she glanced up and spied him. She closed the Bible and set it blindly on the small table beside her. "I didn't realize you were there!"

He chuckled softly. "When a woman is in the presence of the King and three cherubs, a man may as well be invisible."

A soft smile lit her face. "Now all of the wee ones are fat as cherubs, aren't they? 'Tis a welcome sight."

"Seeing you read the Word is every bit as wonderful." He tore his gaze from her before he embarrassed them both. He set the nappies on the table. "Where's Mary? I thought she was helping you."

"I let her go to the stables. Duncan said Blackie is whelping, and Mary wanted to see the puppies right away."

"I hope they hurried. Blackie's had three other litters, and she's quick about it. I suppose Mary and Duncan are claiming one apiece."

"Oh, no! Surely not!" Emily gave him a shocked look. "Duncan knows better than to expect such a thing!"

"Ahh, I understand," John nodded sagely. He paused for effect and fought a smile. "Duncan knows you get pick of the litter, Emily."

Emily spluttered, then started to giggle.

Mary dashed back to the door and announced breathlessly, "There's seven of 'em!"

John crossed the floor and picked up Gracie's babe. "Em, grab Timothy. Mary, you take Violet, and let's get going. I want to see the puppies, too!"

Emily gave him a scandalized look. "I'm thinking I ought not take the babes to such a place."

After making sure he had a firm hold on the baby, John pulled Emily from the chair. He couldn't hide the amusement in his voice. "Emily, our Lord Jesus was born in a stable!"

More giggles spilled out of her.

John felt sure he'd never heard anything half as delightful.

He winked and urged, "Come on!"

Emily whisked the baby out of his arms. "Not yet." She fussed over the babes first. She changed their nappies, cooed to them, and wrapped them in a blanket apiece, regardless of the fact that the sun still shone. She handed Gracie's son back to him.

John chortled. "He looks like a stowaway, hiding in the spare, bundled sails."

They headed toward the stables at more than a genteel walk. In fact, had they each not been slowed down by holding a babe, John wondered if Emily might have actually let go of propriety and skipped a bit. He grinned at the thought, then worried Mary might hasten and be careless.

"Emily, let me carry Timothy, too. You take Violet from Mary, and she can run ahead."

Emily gawked at him, then shook her head. "Now, Mr. Newcomb, 'tis a fine man you are. Not a soul would deny you're capable as can be with clippers and men. Why don't you let me mind cradles and babes?"

He studied her face for a moment, then chuckled in disbelief. "Light as they are, you don't trust me to carry them both, do you?"

She took the babe from Mary, then pursed her lips and looked up at the scudding, white clouds. A second later she trained her gaze on the baby he gently bounced against his shoulder. "Now you're not being fair. I've let you hold Timothy many a time. Much as I love him, you know what a show of trust that is."

"But you're not handing him to me now."

"Let's just say I think you've already plenty enough to handle, holding Gracie's strapping son."

John chortled again. He tilted the baby in his arms back a bit and talked to him. "Now how do you fancy that? You'd best keep that satisfied attitude. If you start crying, Emily won't let me touch the puppies!"

"I won't have to say a word." Emily cast an amused look at him. "Blackie will see to that."

A few minutes later, they sat on the floor of the stable. Duncan let out peals of laughter as the tiny puppies squeaked and wiggled around. He looked up at Emily with huge, shining eyes. "Blackie has seven babies, Em. Seven! Can you just imagine?"

"Aye, and a handsome lot they are," she said.

Duncan wrinkled his nose. "They're funny and wet. I suppose I shouldn't be too surprised you're thinking they're bonny. You said our Timothy was handsome as could be when he got born. I'm glad as ever he doesn't look like he did the first time I saw him!"

John let out a booming laugh at the look on Emily's face. He leaned to the side and scooped Violet from her arms. "Go ahead and set Timmy in the straw next to you. Blackie is uncommonly serene about folks touching her litter as long as they don't lift them away."

In fact, Blackie barely seemed to care that Emily gently stroked a single finger down the back of each puppy. Then again Emily crooned to Blackie the whole while. "Ach! Now aren't you a fine mother? Seven in this pack. You'll be a tired girl, that's for sure. I'm thinking from the looks of them, they've all taken after you—their fur is almost all black as wrought iron."

"It's odd, but some whelps take after their sire while others take after the mother." John meaningfully glanced down at Timothy, then back at her. "That little fellow's got Anna's sweet temperament. I'm certain he's taken after her, clean down to the bone."

Duncan giggled. "Em was just saying last night that

Timothy must take after me because he's always looking for more to eat!"

৵

As Emily braided her hair that night, she remembered John's comment that he needed to discuss something with her. Somehow, in the excitement over looking at the puppies, they'd not had an opportunity to speak. She shrugged. He'd be by in a day or two if it was important.

How she'd come to look forward to the times he stopped by. He filled their cottage with—well, a lot of things. She hadn't meant material things, though he was generous to a fault. No, he brought the important things with him—like safety and courage and companionship. Such a fine man.

He'd taken a shine to Duncan and even let him ride a pony every now and then—but only if he himself was walking alongside. Mr. Peebles, the stable master, had a grandson who was due to come for a visit soon. He and John had decided they'd give both lads riding lessons then.

Nearly half of Duncan's sentences started with "Mr. John says. . . ." For Duncan's not having an older brother or a da to guide him, it did Emily's heart good to see how John Newcomb never made her brother feel like a pest.

Indeed, he never made her feel as if she depended on his charity, either. He allowed her to work so she'd keep her pride and dignity. Others could see 'twas a simple business arrangement, so she never feared for her reputation. Clearly, he would never entertain any true affection for her. She accepted that fact, but in the moments before she fell asleep each night, Emily secretly mourned that she wasn't of his class so things might have worked out between them. Oh, 'twas nothing more than a silly fantasy, but she'd foolishly allowed her heart to weaken toward him. She saw his goodness, his strength, his kindness. She truly enjoyed his companionship. God shone through him, and that mattered most of all. No man would ever look toward her with courting in mind—with Duncan and Timothy in tow, she'd seem like a wallowing barge instead of a sleek clipper.

For all of his kindness, John Newcomb deserved a loving wife and a houseful of healthy sons. Emily wished all that for him, but she knew when that day came, she'd pack up and slip away, because she couldn't quite bear to witness a woman take the place she could never even dream to hold.

The fire had burned too hot late this evening, and her room felt stuffy. Instead of adding a log to last the night, Emily decided to let the end of the fire die out. The bright red sailors' sunset promised tomorrow would be a bonny day.

She fed Timothy one last time, changed his nappy, and tucked him in. After pulling the covers up to Duncan's neck, Emily returned to her bedchamber and knelt at the side of the bed. After a quiet prayer, she slipped into bed and fell asleep.

A bang startled her awake hours later. Emily bolted upright and wished she'd kept some of the fire so she could see better. She crept from the bed and hastily wrapped her shawl about her shoulders.

High-pitched giggles mingled with muffled footsteps. The bedroom door swung wide open, and a candle illuminated a man with a woman clinging to his arm.

"Edward!" Emily gasped.

fourteen

"Hurry, Sir. Hurry! Em needs you!"

Duncan's shout echoed through the house as John dashed down the stairs. He'd barely thrown on his trousers and a shirt and run to see what led the lad to be so upset. Duncan stood in the doorway next to Goodhew, the butler.

Just then one of the stable hands ran up the steps and announced breathlessly, "Someone came to the little house!"

John had ordered Mr. Peebles to assign someone to keep an eye on the caretaker's cottage at all times. The fact that the dwelling had been used made him suspicious, and he'd worried most of all for Emily's safety if whoever had been trysting there should show up again.

Goodhew looked horrified. His nightshirt flapped about him, making him look like an albatross on takeoff as he spun about and pulled a gun from the drawer.

"Keep Duncan here." John grabbed the gun, ran down the steps, and vaulted onto the horse the stable hand had arrived on.

A three-quarter moon lit his way, and he rode down the drive, straight into Emily's small yard. He didn't bother to knock or announce himself; he burst in.

A woman sat on the settee, boo-hooing with great gusto. John barely paid her any heed because he heard foul curses coming from the other room. He followed the small yellow nimbus of light into Emily's bedchamber. "Emily!"

"Here!" she cried back.

Emily held a fireplace poker with both hands. Back against

the wall, Edward held a candlestick in one hand and a wicked-looking knife in the other. He ignored John's arrival and continued to bellow at Emily.

"Emily!" John commanded. "Step out of the room."

"It's him. He's the one."

John wasn't sure whether fear or rage caused her voice to shake. He shoved his pistol into his waistband as he walked to her, then curled his hand around her shoulder. "I'll handle this."

"John! Get rid of that woman!" Edward made a show of setting the candle on the mantel and letting out a sigh of relief. "She's deranged—probably would have killed me if you hadn't gotten here."

"He's the one, John," Emily croaked. "That's Edward."

"I have no idea what this woman means," Edward protested. "I've never met her before."

Emily let out an outraged sound.

"Emily, step out of here. I'll take care of things." John gently pried the poker from her. "Trust me," he urged under his breath.

"He's got a knife."

"Yes, I can see that."

"Don't trust him."

Edward shoved the knife into a sheath at his waist. "Who is this spitfire, John? Your mistress?"

"You know I don't keep a mistress." Emily hadn't budged an inch. Asking her to leave again wouldn't accomplish a thing, so John set her to the side and stood between her and Edward. For a fleeting second, he thought to order her to check on Duncan, but upon finding his cot vacant, she'd undoubtedly come flying back in a panicked rage. Instead he addressed his words to Edward. "Leave here at once and don't come back."

Edward shoved away from the wall with another expletive.

John grabbed him by the collar and shoved him back again. "Keep a decent tongue in your head."

Edward made a choking sound.

"Report to me first thing in the morning at the shipping office." John flung him to the side and watched his brother scramble away and out of the bedchamber.

"Don't leave me!" the woman from the other room sobbed. The patter of her slippers could be heard following Edward's footfall through the main room and out into the yard.

John turned to Emily. Her eyes glittered in the candlelight. She inched back and shook her head. "You let him go."

"Of course I did." John closed the distance between them and calmly drew her shawl together, then wrapped his arms about her trembling form. "I'll deal with him tomorrow, Emily. I had to get him out of here."

Her tears wet his shirt. "He's the one. He lied again. He said he didn't know me."

"Of course he lied." John did his utmost to keep his temper hidden. Emily needed calming in the worst way. He gently stroked her back. "Don't you understand? I wanted him out of here before the noise woke the baby. I didn't want him to know Timmy is here."

Emily's knees nearly buckled. "Oh, no!"

"Shh." John led her out to the parlor.

John lowered Emily to the settee, then stepped back into the bedchamber and brought out the candle and a blanket. He lit the lamp, then wrapped the blanket around Emily. She caught his sleeve. Both her hand and her voice shook. "I'm thanking you for all you've done for my kin, John Newcomb."

"Emily, hush. We need to plan what to do next."

She turned loose of him, dipped her head, and cleared her throat. "There's nothing left to do. I'll be gone by sunup."

"No!"

She shuddered at the word he roared. Still, she seemed more than firm on her decision. She turned toward the kitchen and raised her voice. "Duncan, come help me. We've packing to see to."

John cupped her chin and forced her to look up at him. The shocked worry in her eyes let him know she hadn't thought about the fact that Edward's shouting had to have awakened the lad. "Duncan is up at my house. He knew he could trust me—he ran to my place so I could come protect you. You can bet I'm going to do just that. You're not running away. You, Duncan, and Timmy belong here."

A sad, all-too-worldly-wise parody of a smile tugged at the corners of her mouth. "We don't belong in your world, John Newcomb, and well you know it. I'm taking my boys off before that dreadful man does something."

"What could he do? Think, Emily."

"Oh, I am. You were, too, when you thought of keeping Edward from finding the baby. Your brother's a rascal—" Her voice broke.

"Ahh, Em." John sat next to her and pulled her into the shelter of his arms. "I'll protect you and the boys."

"You can't," she said in a hopeless tone.

He slowly slid his hand down her hair. Soft little wisps curled about his finger and sprang loose, only to be replaced again and again. The wet warmth of her tears seeped through his shirt, but she didn't weep in torrents. Instead, her tears fell one by one in solitary anguish.

"I'm sorry for what he, uh, believed about"—she barely choked out the word—"mistress."

"You've nothing to be sorry for. Edward is responsible for his own thoughts—lurid and wrong as they may be. He's judging others for his own sin. Ofttimes guilty men do so."

"He h–had another woman—"

"Em, my Em, I'm so sorry." He felt her shudder and knew the impact of Edward's betrayal was hitting full force for the second time. The first time John watched her limp away from the shipyard, and she'd had to handle the blow by herself. This time he'd not let her feel alone.

"I'm supposing I ought to be thankful the Lord didn't let him come barging in with another woman in front of Anna."

"That is something to be thankful for," he allowed, though he felt sick about the whole sordid mess.

"You'll tell Cook, Gracie, and Mary good-bye for me?"

John's arms tightened, crushing her to his chest. "You're staying right here."

She patted him and said in a tearful voice that managed to make pretenses toward soothing, "There, now, I'll be sure to sneak a message to you now and again to let you know how our Timmy's doing."

"You'll do no such thing! Emily, you can't leave. You and Duncan won't ever make it on your own, and who will watch the baby whilst you work? There are far too many problems. I'll not hear of this nonsense."

Emily pushed away and stared at him. The lamplight flickered in her glistening green eyes. "Best you listen and heed me, John Newcomb. I'll not stand by and let that man hurt my family e'er again."

Her spirit pleased him. John brushed a few of her tears away with his thumb. "He won't hurt you. I won't let him."

"You're not listening to me. I don't give a whit about myself. I'm worried about Timothy! What if he tries to take him away?"

"Em, Edward is too footloose to want to be tied down to a babe. Besides, there's no church record naming Edward as the father."

"Oh, sure and enough, he might not try to nab a babe; but give him a few years, and he could well change his tune. He's got the morals of an alley cat and the heart of a snake." She shook her head. "No. 'Tis a risk I won't take."

"Do you trust me?"

Emily drew the blanket around herself and stood. She paced away, then turned. Her mouth opened, then shut without her uttering a word.

John met her gaze unflinchingly. For all she'd been through, she had every reason not to trust another soul. Nonetheless, he wanted—no, he needed—her to trust him.

Emily turned away. "Forgive me, John. I'm not sure what to think right now. If ever a man has shown himself to be dependable and Christian, 'tis you. You're asking me to rely on your say-so, and my head tells me I can. But 'tisn't you I hold concerns about, and your brother already proved he leaves a heart load of grief and worry in his wake."

"I understand, Emily, but—"

"You have to admit you were blind to your brother's ways. You defended him." Her voice went hushed. "Even when Anna longed to be acknowledged as his wife, you never allowed her that. You'd never knowingly let him hurt us, but brotherly love veiled the truth back then. I can't help but worry that I'll rely on your word and it will happen again."

John sat there and let her speak. She'd not spoken out of bitterness. Her words came from the ache and worries he wanted to share, so he'd listen as she spilled them.

"I don't trust Edward for a single minute. Anna's gone, and he's rich. He could pay a judge, just as he paid someone to pretend to be a parson. Even if he didn't want Timmy for himself, what if he tried to take him and give him to someone else?"

Silence filled the room. Emily gave John a look of resignation; yet she somehow managed to square her shoulders. "I'd best spend my night praying. You'll know when I've made up my mind."

John stood and nodded. He crossed the room and tugged the blanket even tighter around her. "I've no doubt they've tucked Duncan in up at my house. Let's take the baby on up there, too."

"Your brother will be up at the big house. I'm thinking my brother belongs back here with me."

"You're not thinking of slipping away in the middle of the night, are you?"

Emily stared at him. She chewed on her lip for a brief moment, then sighed. "I'd be telling a fearsome lie if I said the thought never crossed my mind."

"You've never once lied to me, Em. Give me your word you'll stay here—at least for tonight."

She shuddered. "I can't give you my word, John. If I do, what will I do if he comes back here tonight?"

"Em," he said softly as he tucked a strand of her soft hair behind her left ear, "why didn't you just tell me you were afraid he'd come back here tonight?"

She hitched one shoulder. "I suppose I'm not in the practice of whispering my worries to another."

He turned her by the shoulders, snatched up the lamp, and marched her back into the bedchamber. "Get dressed; then we'll talk."

"We've talked plenty. Sometimes it's best to stop talking and act."

Aware she had yet to give her promise that she wouldn't run off, John bent over, took Timothy from his cradle, and clasped him to his shoulder as he straightened. "I'm taking action, Em. Timmy-boy and I'll be in the other room."

A few moments later, the door opened, and Emily emerged from the bedchamber. Lamplight turned her hair to a molten gold and burnished copper combination. She'd gotten over enough of the shock that color now stained her cheeks.

John admired Emily for her character qualities. On several occasions he'd caught her at prayer or reading her Bible and appreciated the devotion she held for the Lord. Her wit and spunk amused him, too. Many times he'd even considered her hair to be lovely, and the day he bought her dress, he distinctly thought of what a lovely woman she was. . .but at that moment, he looked at her in a completely different light. He couldn't hope to have a better ally in the troubled days ahead than this beautiful woman.

Emily crossed the floor and set the lamp on a small table. She knelt on the floor and silently reached up to take possession of the baby. Worried, even frightened as she was, her features softened with love as her fingertips grazed the blanket. She didn't say a word. Just the way she tilted her head a bit to the side and raised her brows silently invited John to relinquish Timothy.

Instead John's arm curled a bit more tightly around the boy. He reached over with his other hand and slid it over hers, pressing it against the babe. "Em, we're in this together."

She focused on him. Even in the lamplight, he could see her eyes darken. A brave, sad smile fleetingly lifted the corners of her mouth. "If ever God made a fine man, surely 'tis you, John Newcomb." The smile disappeared, and she continued. "But 'tisn't right for me to depend on you or anyone else. This is my problem."

"Why is it any more your problem than it is mine?"

"Anna was my sister." Tears filled her voice and eyes.

"Aye, and she was a lovely, innocent young girl," John agreed softly. He curled his fingers to hold her hand more firmly. "But Edward is my brother. His dishonor caused this, so betwixt you and me, I'm more responsible for trying to right this as much as possible."

"I'll be disagreeing with you, John Newcomb. Most certainly I will. Anna gave Timmy into my keeping. He's mine. We both know full well that I'm far better able to handle this wee babe than you are to manage your brother. I can slip away, land a job, and make a new life. There's not a thing you could do if he comes here and takes Timmy."

"Enough of this." Her words burned his soul. John broke contact with her and stood. "Toss whatever you need for the bedtime and some nappies into a pillow slip. You and Timothy are to be my guests tonight."

"Ach! We cannot do that!" She scrambled to her feet. "Have you not been listening? The scoundrel you call a brother is in that very house. I'll not stay under the same roof with him."

"I can be every bit as obstinate as you. Now you have a choice: You come with me, and we'll settle you in a room along with one of the maids so all proprieties will be observed; or I'll stay here the whole night long, and though we'll behave with the morals of pure saints, we'll scandalize the whole town, and your reputation will be in shreds. Take your pick, Emily O'Brien."

She glowered, then marched into the bedchamber. John stood in the doorway and watched as she grabbed a pillow and shook the feathered sack from it with notable temper. As she stuffed a nightdress and the shawl he'd given her into it, she muttered, "Every last angel and saint in heaven is likely blushing at your words, you rogue."

John chuckled. "I don't think they are, but you've turned a fetching shade of pink."

"I'm thinking you ought to make yourself useful, John Newcomb." She snapped a diaper in the air, then folded it. "Go fetch some breeches for Duncan."

ea

She'd never been in such a grand home. Emily barely set foot in the foyer of John's place, then turned and bumped into him as she tried to exit.

"Did you forget something?" He tossed the pillow slip onto the beautiful marble floor.

"I forgot my wits," she muttered.

"You're never witless." John chuckled and tried to turn her around, but she didn't budge.

"I don't belong here. I'll wait outside whilst you send someone to fetch Duncan."

"Sir?" A tall man who managed to sound and look dignified in his nightshirt and robe stood by the open door.

"Goodhew, this is Miss Emily O'Brien. You've seen her nephew, Timothy, already. They're to be our guests tonight."

"Very well, Sir. Eloise already prepared the blue suite, just in case." Goodhew shut the front door.

Emily wanted to moan at the loss of her exit.

"It's a pleasure to meet you, Miss Emily." The butler's tone carried a touch of warmth as he nodded polite acknowledgment of the introduction. He then turned back to John. "I took the liberty of setting a fire in the study so you could warm up, Sir. Cook will bring in a light repast for you both as soon as you're settled."

Emily felt stuck. She searched for a way or excuse to leave, but her mind went blank.

John took her in hand and piloted her into the study as if she were a barge going through rough waters. Once there, she halted on a plush, ornate carpet. "I–I can't go in here," she whispered. "I didn't wipe my feet."

"Neither did I. Just step out of your slippers."

It wasn't until then Emily looked down. "Mr. John! You're—"

"Just leave the tray by the fire, Cook. Thank you for getting that ready." John's words cut Emily's observation short. He took the baby from her arms.

"Will you need anything special for the baby, Miss Emily?" Goodhew asked.

Emily tried not to gawk at him. She wasn't accustomed to being treated like a society lady. She stammered, "I give him milk and molasses."

"There's no need for that." Cook took Timothy from John and turned to Emily. "I'll take him on up to your room and feed him."

"Thank you, Cook." John tugged Emily over to a chair by the roaring fire and said under his breath, "Let her take him upstairs, Em. I don't expect Edward to come home tonight, but if he does, we'll want the baby hidden."

Goodhew slipped in from a side door and escorted Cook out. Emily stared at them, then turned to look at the ceiling-high bookcases that went around three of the walls.

John gently pushed Emily into a huge leather chair that nearly swallowed her.

Satisfied Timothy was in good hands, she then stared back down at John's bare feet. "If you point me to the kitchen, I'll get you a kettle of warm water. We'll wash your feet, and that'll warm them straight away."

"The fire will do." He eased into a chair and stuck his legs out straight. "I wouldn't complain if you served me some of that cake. It's one of Cook's specialties."

Calling upon the memories of the times she'd helped Mama serve guests at Master Reilly's house, Emily made a plate for him and also prepared his tea according to the preferences she'd already noted he held. *Odd, how I know such details about this man.*

After she served him, she perched on the edge of her chair.

"Emily, eat," John bade her quietly. "Put extra honey in the tea—it's good for your shock."

"I can't eat, so it's silly for me to fill a plate," she said simply. "It's not right for me to waste good food."

"You're here tonight. Refusing to eat or sleep won't help any. We need to be certain you are at your best to deal with things in the morning."

"I don't know what I'll do tomorrow—in fact, I don't even know what to do right now!"

"Let's have you rest." He held up his hand to keep her from interrupting him. "You and the boys are perfectly safe here. I can't even be sure if Edward will come home at all. If he does, he'll be in the other wing, so he won't have any notion at all that you're here."

"So you'd hide us in plain sight?"

He chuckled softly. "Cleverly put."

She watched him eat the cake in a few large bites. The fire crackled and popped, making the vast room seem cozy. Fearing he'd catch her staring at him, Emily looked at the portion of the room the fire illuminated. Master Reilly's home didn't begin to compare with the splendor of this place. At first glance everything was imposing, but another look changed her mind. Someone had taken care to add details that made this huge place a welcoming home. Every so often, on the bottom shelves, a child's toy sat next to the books. Portraits weren't strictly of stern-faced men and women—there were several of children with pets.

"See the framed picture to the right of the mantel?" John broke into her musings. "I did that when I was Duncan's age. I'd taken a mind to help myself to my father's inkwell and pen."

Emily gasped. The result hung there—plain as could be. A sheet of foolscap with a spill of ink and several fingerprints had been framed and displayed as if it were a Flemish master's work.

John chuckled. "Oh, the desk was a horrible mess, and my parents were justifiably angry. Grandfather came in just about then and roared with laughter. Without saying a word, he set aside the paper and peeled up the red felt on the blotter. There, on the leather beneath it, was a very old splotch of ink that had faded into a bluish tone. My father had done the self-same thing when he was a lad, too."

Emily flashed him a smile. "So you were a rapscallion?"

"No more so than any other lad. Grandfather saved my 'picture' and hung it here. He told me it was a reminder that whatever trouble a man does, it leaves a blot on his soul. My father's blot was covered by red felt—and Grandfather chose red instead of green, because he thought it represented how the blood of Christ covers the blots of sin on our souls. It's a peculiarity in this home—you'll not see any green felt on the desks. It's all red."

"What a lovely lesson."

John nodded and rose. "You're weary. Let's get you settled in for what's left of the night." He padded over to the serving tray and cut a generous slice of cake. To Emily's surprise, he shoved the plate into her hands. "You just may want to nibble later. Now come with me."

Emily got halfway up the wide, sweeping staircase before she stopped cold. "Oh, no!"

"What's wrong?"

"My Bible!"

"You can borrow mine for the night."

She shook her head. " 'Tisn't just that. The marriage license and the matrimony page are in the Bible. If Edward goes back to the cottage. . ."

"I'll take care of it." John nudged her up the stairs and stopped outside an open door. "Wait here. I'll fetch you my Bible."

Emily did as he bade. Moments later, John handed her his Bible with the lovely gold-leaf pages. "Will you be able to sleep?"

She shrugged. "I can't say. My body's weary, but my heart and soul are doing a jig."

John cupped her cheek and looked at her tenderly. "Then read Luke chapter twelve, verses six and seven."

Emily looked at him and nodded. With him touching her so kindly, she couldn't manage to speak.

"Sweet dreams." He walked back down the stairs, and Emily knew he'd left to go fetch her Bible.

His heavy Bible rested in her hands, almost as heavily as the burdens in her heart. She knew she needed to do something quickly to safeguard precious little Timmy. Duncan, too—because she didn't want him to see Edward Newcomb and know he was the wicked man who had tricked them all.

Lord, I don't know what to do. You know how scared I am. I love Timmy, and I'm sore afraid I won't be able to protect him from Edward. You'll have to give me a message. I'm not asking for anything grand—just a place I can take my boys and live peacefully. Reveal Your plan to me and calm my fretful heart.

Cook tucked Timmy into a cradle, then slipped out of the room. Emily sat on the edge of a beautiful four-poster bed and sighed. John hadn't once mentioned how she'd been shaking. Aye, and she had been—from the moment she heard the noise, clear up 'til now. It took every shred of her courage to make her voice sound stable, but her hands jittered like a blade of grass in a stiff wind. How kind of John to loan her his Bible.

Tired as she was, Emily knew she'd not be able to sleep a wink. Memories of Edward surfaced—of his wooing Anna, of how sour he'd been to discover he had a child on the way, of tonight when he'd pulled out that horrifying knife.

After all that, how can John expect me to sleep? The weight of the Bible in her hands commanded her attention. Since John had recommended a particular passage, she turned to it.

Are not five sparrows sold for two farthings, and not one of them is forgotten before God? But even the very hairs of your head are all numbered. Fear not therefore: ye are of more value than many sparrows.

Emily stared at the verses and blinked. She'd just told God how scared she was. He'd known it even before she prayed and in His infinite wisdom and love used John to urge her to read these very words for comfort.

Her pulse slowed, and the weight on her shoulders lifted as she read the words once more. After she set the Bible on the bedside table, a maid came in.

"Miss Emily, I'm Clara. I'm to spend the night with you and the wee one. I just checked in on Duncan. He's next door, and he's sleepin' heavy as an anchor."

They spoke a few minutes; then Emily went behind the screen and changed into her bed gown. Once she came out, she peeped at Timmy, then crept into the huge bed. The feather pillow and comforters enveloped her. . .just like the little sparrows in God's hands.

fifteen

Emily woke the next morning to soft, musical crooning. She opened her eyes slowly and watched as John's laundress suckled the baby. During the night, Clara had slept in the room on a fainting couch. She'd insisted Emily sleep, that she had plenty of experience with her younger brothers and sisters. She'd deftly mixed the milk and molasses, so Emily hesitantly agreed, with the caveat that if Timothy got stubborn, she was to be awakened.

Timmy and the maid must have gotten along famously. In fact, he seemed quite content now with Gracie, too. Emily yawned and blinked.

Gracie chortled softly. "I'll wager you've not slept more than a few hours at a time. It was that way right after I had my son."

"I didn't even hear you come in!"

"That's because you needed the sleep. Mr. John says you're to laze in bed awhile."

"Duncan—"

"Your little brother scampered down to the stable. Mary went with him. Blackie's puppies have us all charmed."

Emily sat up and stretched. In the morning light, this room looked like a little corner of heaven. The blue walls and the fluffy blue-and-white bedding made her feel as if she were floating on a cloud, and sunbeams coming through the far window made all of the golden accents glow. "Mercy! I was so weary last night that I didn't even take note of how beautiful this is. Mayhap I ought to see if I sprouted wings during the night, to be waking in such a place as this," she marveled.

Gracie laughed as she fastened her bodice. "It's pretty as can be. You rest on back. Soon as I get downstairs, I'll tell Teresa to send up your tray."

"Tray? Oh, no." Emily hopped out of bed. "I'm no high-born woman to be waited upon."

"Mr. John ordered it."

Emily grabbed her day gown and slipped behind a dressing screen. "Mr. John's a fine man, but he's got the wrong notion. I've never been waited on in my life."

Gracie chuckled softly. "Mr. John ordered us all to pamper you. You may as well give in graciously."

"We both know good and well I have plenty to do today. Sitting about is pure foolishness. Now where is your wee son?"

"Cook has him in the kitchen. He's gumming a biscuit she made for him. He'll be in a fine temper if you try to sweep him away before he eats half a dozen. Her own wee one is lying in a box on the table, cooing at her while she kneads bread."

Emily came out from behind the screen and started to brush her hair.

"Oh, Miss Emily! Your hair is pretty as can be!"

"Thank you." Emily rebraided it with the intent of putting it up into a cornette, but she suddenly stopped short. "Well, mercy. I didn't think to bring along any hairpins."

A tentative knock sounded on the door. Emily startled, then began to cross the room. Gracie called out merrily, "Come on in!"

Goodhew opened the door and stood at the threshold. "Miss Emily, you're awake. Mr. John ordered Cook to make you a breakfast tray. I'll have Teresa bring it right up. After you're finished, he'd like to meet with you in the study."

"There's no call to be fussing over me. I'll follow you to

the kitchen, if you'd be so kind as to show me the way."

"Very well, Miss."

&

John heard a baby cry and smiled. He'd arranged everything so Clara and Gracie would shift in and out of Emily's bedchamber so she could catch up on a bit of sleep. Clearly they'd slipped little Timothy out and brought him down here.

Upstairs his housekeeper and three of the maids were cleaning the nursery. He'd already inspected it and found it to be satisfactory, but Mrs. Thwaite clucked and tutted about its needing to be dusted and aired. Knowing her, she'd have it so royalty could eat off the windowsill.

As long as the *Cormorant* was docked and Edward was in town, John determined to keep Emily, Duncan, and Timothy here. He could come up with no better way to protect them. Emily could spend the days in the sunny nursery with Cook and Gracie's babes and Timothy. A safe place with a crib and toys, the children would fare well there, and Emily would feel securely tucked away. The moment she came downstairs, he'd fill her in on his plan. As for her future—well, he'd broach that subject later.

In the meantime, he needed to see to other matters. First and foremost, he needed to deal with Edward. For all of his prayers, he had yet to sense any direction to take or words of wisdom to apply. Simply put, all he felt was rage.

What should I do? Edward is my brother, my own flesh and blood. But so is Baby Timothy—and he's innocent. Edward made his own choices; Timothy doesn't deserve to live in poverty because of his father's sins. John rested his elbow on the desk and pinched the bridge of his nose, wishing he could be rid of this entire headache.

In that moment, when his eyes were closed, something rustled. Someone tugged on his sleeve. "Mr. John!"

John opened his eyes and turned. "Yes, Duncan?"

"I seen him. He's here. Down by the stable with Edward."

"Who?"

"The parson who came to my house and married Anna and Edward. He's here! You can ask him. He'll prove our Anna was really married!"

John stood, and Duncan tugged on his sleeve more urgently. "Please hurry."

They exited by the doors leading to the garden, and John lengthened his stride. Duncan galloped alongside him to keep pace.

"Are you sure he's the one?" he asked the boy.

"Aye, that I am. Only he's not wearing the same clothes this time. He looks like a fancy man instead of a churchy one. This way—they went 'round back, over by the extra water trough."

John stepped over a fence and lifted Duncan after him, then hastened on. What was Edward up to? Obviously it wasn't anything good, or he'd be doing it out in the open instead of behind the stables. John rounded the corner just in time to see a man mount a dappled gelding and ride off.

"Oh, no! He's going away," Duncan moaned.

Edward turned toward them. "Out for your morning constitutional, Brother?"

John glared at him. The man Duncan thought to be a priest was a notorious slave trader. "What are you doing, meeting with Phineas Selsior?"

"That's my business, not yours."

Duncan shouted. "He's the priest who married you to my Anna!"

Edward sneered. "Honestly, John. What are you doing, associating with these bilge rats?"

"You said you loved Anna!" Duncan cried. "You married her."

"Shh, Duncan." John drew the boy close, and the lad

wrapped his arms about John's leg and held fast like a barnacle.

"We'll talk in the study, Edward." John could barely hold his temper. How dare his brother call Emily and her family bilge rats? And what business did he have with Phineas Selsior?

Edward shoved his hands into his pockets and shrugged. "There's nothing to discuss. You can stow that 'brother's keeper' nonsense. I'm a grown man, and I'll attend to my own business."

"You didn't mind your own business. You abandoned your wife."

"I have absolutely no idea what you're talking about." Edward leaned against a nearby tree trunk. He smirked. "I've never walked down the aisle."

'Twasn't in a church wedding, but I overlooked that because we were both wedging the ceremony in the few minutes betwixt our shifts of work. Emily's words echoed in John's mind. It sickened him to think of the lengths his brother had gone to, to delude them.

Suddenly, the verse from Matthew flashed through his mind. *"And if thine eye offend thee, pluck it out, and cast it from thee: it is better for thee to enter into life with one eye, rather than having two eyes to be cast into hell fire."* He knew it then. He had to cast his brother aside.

"You're to leave and never come back. I'll have Goodhew pack your personal belongings."

Edward negligently lifted a shoulder, as if it meant nothing to him.

"You'll no longer captain the *Cormorant,* either." John watched his brother's face go florid.

"You're wrong! She's mine!"

John shook his head. "You know full well she's mine." He looked off to the side where Selsior had ridden off, then looked back at Edward. "You've used her to bring in slaves, haven't you?"

"Not from the outside—just trading within our boundaries. All perfectly legal. Lucrative, too."

"Not with any of my vessels."

"Being self-righteous never filled your pockets." Edward pushed away from the tree and stalked closer to John. "Half of the shipping business, half of those ships, should belong to me. Grandfather changed his will because he found out I'd brought back a pair of slaves my first run out as Enoch's first mate. Bad enough I lived through the indignity of his leaving me to play lackey to old Enoch. I figured he'd punished me more than enough. The day the will was read and I learned how he'd cheated me of my birthright, I decided the Newcomb name meant nothing. I've used your ship to do as I jolly well pleased, and I've earned a tidy sum for it, too. Slaves bring good money—a hundred for a brat, four or five hundred for a breeding woman, and up to eight hundred for a strapping worker with some brains. Selsior gives me a full third of the cut."

John stared at him. "No more."

"Oh, that's where you're wrong. It didn't take much snooping. I saw the grave at the church. The headstone holds only one name—Anna's. There's no mention of an infant buried with her. Then I went back to the cottage. There's a cradle there."

John's blood ran cold.

"All I had to do was ask a few questions. Folks think Anna was married to a ship's captain—funny, no one knew who. You're going to deal with me. I get the *Cormorant*. In exchange, I keep my mouth shut, and no one will know that baby is a bast—"

"Enough!" John roared. He stared at his brother with absolute loathing.

"It's your choice. You know it is. He can grow up respectably, or I can make sure everyone knows he's—shall we say—'from the wrong side of the blanket'?"

"You're a wicked, wicked man!" Duncan cried.

"I always thought you were a clever lad." Edward sneered at the lad, then sauntered off.

Duncan couldn't hide his tears. "What are you going to do, Mr. John?"

John knelt and hugged the boy. "I'll have to pray about it."

"Em was wrong."

"What was she wrong about?"

Duncan sniffled and gave John a woebegone look. "She says the devil brings cookies. Edward is evil, but he never brought cookies."

❧

John calmed Duncan and left him in the care of the stable master. "Our littlest stable hand had a bad start to the day. Perhaps you could help him turn it around with a nice riding lesson."

"A fine idea!" Mr. Peebles rubbed his hands together.

Duncan looked up at John. "Are you going to go take care of Em and Timmy?"

"Aye, and you can be sure things will work out."

The lad stared at him somberly for a long count, then nodded once. "You never lied to us. Edward did, but you never have."

John lifted him to stand on a bale of hay. He stared him in the eye and pledged, "I'll always tell you the truth. Things are going to change. You don't have to worry. Before I go into the house, do you want to pray with me?"

"All right. Maybe I'd better pray now. You can save your prayer 'til you're with Sis."

Duncan dipped his head and folded his hands. John folded his big hands over Duncan's little ones. They bowed their heads until their foreheads touched.

"Dear God, I know I prayed hard and lots to have You bring Edward back, but I've changed my mind. Please make him go far away forever. Don't let him take our Timmy. Help Mr. John to be strong and brave. And, God, please bless Em and me so we don't have to go back to the way things used to be. Amen."

John squeezed Duncan's hands. For a moment he couldn't speak. Finally, his voice husky, he said, "That was a fine prayer."

As he walked back to the house, John let out a huge sigh. Aye, from the mouth of that little lad had come a prayer that said everything he'd been feeling, too. *Lord, give me wisdom. Guide me to do the right things.*

Inside his home, John followed Goodhew's tip and went to the nursery. Once he reached the doorway, he stopped. Emily had Timothy in one arm and Gracie's son in her other. Her back turned to the door, she was singing a little ditty he'd never heard before, and the lilt in her voice had both babes cooing. She moved with grace as she dipped from one side to the other in time with her song.

The nursery sparkled. So did she. It looked so right with babies in it; she looked so natural holding babies in her arms. Someday he wanted his own children in this nursery. *Our children.* The thought stunned him.

Suddenly he felt like a sailor who'd come home after a long voyage. How had he failed to see what was before him all these days? From his frustrations with her the first day, to his concerns, to his caring—why shouldn't it be a natural step to have come to love her?

Lord, thank You for her. Thank You for taking the blinders off so I could see Your plan for us.

"Emily?"

"Oh!" She startled and wheeled around. "Mr. John! I went

down to your study, but you'd left."

"I had a bit of unexpected business. I need to speak with you. Will you walk with me?"

"But the babies—"

"I'm sure most of the staff will volunteer to mind them."

Emily smiled. "Ach, now there's a truth spoken too mildly. I went down to the kitchen, and every last lass there was willing to rob me of my wee ones."

John chuckled. "They're not the only ones. I fancy Goodhew embarrasses himself by neglecting his image in favor of spoiling the babies."

They quickly arranged for the babies to be minded; then John led Emily out of the house. She silently walked alongside him until they reached the crest of the hill. Once there, John looked out at the horizon and smiled. "Fair weather and a sound wind. My ships will make good distance today."

Emily pulled the edges of her shawl closer and huddled in its cover. She averted her gaze to the small stand of trees to their left.

"Are you cold?" John started to unbutton his jacket at once.

"No, no. I'm fine."

His fingers stopped, and he gave her a quizzical look. "What's wrong?"

She hitched her shoulder and remained mute.

He unfastened the last button, shrugged out of his coat, and stepped behind her. The heavy fabric enveloped her. It carried his warmth and scent. John folded his arms high across her shoulders and rested his chin on her head. The weight forced her to rest her chin on his arms. The hold felt strange—companionable, warm, and undemanding, but safe in a way she couldn't imagine.

"Look out there," he coaxed in his velvety baritone. "Take a moment to appreciate the beauty. The ocean is one of God's richest masterpieces. It's always there, but never the same." He inhaled deeply, and his vast chest pressed against her back. "The salt tang is invigorating. Aye, 'tis. Just look at how the sunlight skips on the waves to turn them silver and gold. When you feel troubled, walk here, Emily. Gaze out at this, and let it give you peace."

She shuddered in his arms. He eased his hold and turned her around. Brows knit, he studied her. "What is it?"

"The sea gives you peace. For me, 'tisn't the case at all. When I look at it, all I see are countless miles of water, and every last one keeps me from my da and ma. You see the silver and gold because you make your living on the water. I smell the salt of all the tears I've cried in fear and sorrow."

She tried to give him a brave smile and shrug, as if those feelings no longer bothered her. Suddenly the weight of his coat almost felt like the pressure of all the burdens she shouldered.

"Aw, Emily," he crooned. His expression softened with compassion. Gently he cradled her jaw in his big hand and studied her in silence.

She wanted to look away. Already he knew far too much about her. Life had denied her any privacy or dignity. The last thing she wanted was for him to sense how lost and alone she felt, but something about his eyes kept her staring up at him.

"I'm sorry, little one. I—"

She pulled away. "No. Oh, no, you needn't be sorry for me. I'm not to be pitied. Duncan and I have each other, and we're doing fine with little Timothy."

"Of course you've done well with Timothy."

"He's a grand man-child—growing bigger by the day."

"Be that as it may, Emily, you're entitled to want something for yourself."

"What with the other wee one I care for, my days are full,

and I want for neither bread nor shelter. Besides—"

"Hush!" He stepped closer and held her shoulders.

She wanted to squirm away from his hold, away from his piercing gaze and the way he made her long for the things she'd missed and could never have. He saw straight through the list of things she'd spouted. Yes, she truly meant she felt grateful for each and every one of them; but John seemed to hone in on the things she lacked, and she couldn't allow him to see the holes in her heart and soul. Most of all, she didn't want him to see the longing in her eyes. What woman wouldn't fall in love with a man like him? *Aye, but I'm ordinary, and he's extraordinary. I'm a fool even to think of this.*

"Emily, have you never longed for what other young women want?"

She tore her gaze from him and stared at his cravat. The laugh she forced sounded hollow, even to her own ears. The question made her ache something awful. Of all the men in the world, why did he have to ask? "What would that be? A child? I've two to rear. Boys, the both of them—and that is always what is most desired."

"What of a husband, a home, and beautiful clothes?"

She tilted her head to the side and gathered enough courage to meet his eyes once again. "Men rarely are worth much trouble, if you'll pardon my saying so. The landowner back home split apart all the families under his care without so much as flinching. Da couldn't keep his own children. Even here most of the men go off to sea and leave their wives behind to tend to the wearing realities of life. A good many of the seamen drink away their pay long afore they make it home."

"I can't contest the fact that you've seen more than your share of men who are rascals, Emily. Don't you know any who are decent, hard-working, God-fearing men?"

Only you, John Newcomb, she thought. Instead she tore her

gaze from him and stared at the ground. "We both know there's not a man in five counties who'd ever look at me. I'm poor, uneducated, and have two lads he'd have to feed. I gave up dreaming years ago, John Newcomb. Dreams are for fools and children."

"Emily, you're wrong."

"Please don't feel obliged to give me any fancy words or promise I'll turn a corner and find true love. I decided long ago that it all came down to me relying on God to get me through each day. Whether due to intent or circumstance, others will end up letting me down. Edward was a scoundrel; Da couldn't keep us." She shrugged, then cleared her throat. "Aye, I know God will never fail me, so He's where I'm putting my trust."

"Joshua chapter one, verse nine: 'Have not I commanded thee? Be strong and of a good courage; be not afraid, neither be thou dismayed: for the Lord thy God is with thee whithersoever thou goest,' " John quoted softly.

Emily nodded. "Aye, now there you have it. 'Tis a verse I cherish, too. It's seen me through many a hard day, and God is always faithful to be there for me."

"Em, what if a man *wanted* to be in your life?"

Deep inside she winced at that question. Of all men, why did John Newcomb—the man she loved and could never have—ask her that? He unerringly hit her weak spots in this conversation. Unwilling to let him read any of her thoughts, she turned back to stare at the ocean. "A man who wants to start off his life with the likes of me and the boys? There is no such man, one willing to take on what he'd consider such burdens."

John stepped closer. She shivered ever so slightly beneath his coat. He gently tugged her shawl from beneath the jacket and draped it about her head and shoulders. Emily wasn't sure whether he'd chosen to stand between her and the ocean to arrest her view or block the wind. As his hands brought the edges of the shawl beneath her chin, he nudged her to look up at him.

"They're not burdens, Emily. Though the responsibilities have weighed heavily on you, you've never considered caring for your family a burden."

She smiled at him. "Love lightened the load."

"Emily." He slipped his rough hands up to cup her face, and his voice dropped to a deeper register. "God has given me that same love for you and your little family—I'll gladly take on such precious 'burdens.' "

"And I'm thanking you for having done so. You've been a true blessing."

"No, Em." He rubbed her cheek with his thumb and smiled. "I'm not talking about the little things I did to help you out. I'm talking about the future."

Why was he touching her like this? He'd been a comforting friend in the past, but this—it felt softer, more personal. . .like a caress. Her wits scattered in the wind. Emily stared at his cravat again. "Only God knows the future. The arrangement we have for now is wondrous, though. I do love minding the babes."

"Woman!" He said the word in an odd tone that hinted at both humor and exasperation.

Emily looked up at his face again.

His thumb slid over her lips. "I'm not trying to discuss a business arrangement. I'm asking you to be my wife!"

John watched as Emily's eyes glistened suspiciously. Her lips parted in shock, and the color drained from her face. She bowed her head, and he could see the tips of her russet lashes flutter as she blinked away tears.

"Emily?"

"John, you don't have to do this. Truly you don't."

"I know I don't. I'm asking you to be my wife because it's

what I want." She still wouldn't look him in the eye. He sensed her emotional withdrawal and could bear it. He'd not let go, and he could feel the pulse by her jaw thundering beneath his fingertips.

"You don't owe us a thing. You've been generous, but just because Edward—"

"Edward has nothing to do with this."

"You bear no responsibility, no fault. I'm so sad that you'd do this to try to mend some of his wrongs."

"I'm not."

"You're doing it to protect Timmy, then, aren't you? What did your brother try to do?"

John tilted her face up to his. "Emily, this will shelter Timmy, but that's simply a bonus. As for my brother—I've ordered Goodhew to pack all of Edward's possessions. Edward won't be living here, and he's banned from any of my vessels."

"Oh, no! John, I lost my sister—must you lose your brother, too?"

"There is no other way," he said grimly. "No man is beyond the grace or redemption of God. I'll pray for Edward, but until he repents and seeks salvation, he's not welcome here."

"He put great store by the *Cormorant*. Surely he kicked up a mighty fuss over that." Pain streaked across her face. "Now you're proposing. What did he—"

He gave her a tender smile. "As if anything Edward might say matters at all."

"But—"

"Emily, from the first time I saw you, you caught my attention. Duncan charmed me, and I felt compassion for Anna—but you—you were different. Your spirit drew me. I finally came to realize why you've captivated me. I've not married because I never found a woman who I felt would be a suitable partner."

"I'm far from suitable! I'm poor—"

"Shh." He gently pressed his fingers to her lips. "Money can be made and spent, won and lost. Your wealth is superior, Emily. You have a wealth of love to share. Other women have looked at my business with a greedy eye—but they also knew my business forces me to deal with rough, rowdy men. In their presence I have to pretend that part of my life doesn't exist. When I marry, I want a woman who is my life partner— my helpmeet. One who isn't afraid of the rugged side I have."

Emily turned her head to free herself. "Oh, but, John, you're rich as King Midas himself! I'm telling you, that scares me silly. I wouldn't fit in as your wife here in your own house, let alone in society!"

"Love makes things work, and I have a heart full of love for you, Emily." He captured her hands and brought them up to his lips. He kissed the backs of her fingers. "Tell me you care for me. Agree to be my beloved bride."

"I do love you, John Newcomb. I love you straight down to the bottom of my heart. I just didn't imagine God would ever grant that desire because it's so impossible."

"Nothing is impossible with God." He drew her into his arms. "So I aim to make you my bride. I'll give you three days to get ready."

Her breath caught, but he silenced whatever she was about to say with a kiss.

❧

The next day Emily stood in the heavenly bedroom up in the big house. Down the hall she could hear a slight commotion. When she turned to go tend to it, the dressmaker stopped her. "Don't move!"

Cook laughingly instructed, "Clara, go make sure Lily and Mary are handling the babies. And you, Miss Emily, you'd best hold still as can be. Mr. John ordered me to be sure you

ad a wedding gown worthy of a fairy princess, and I aim to
be sure you do."

Emily looked down at the silver-shot white satin skirts and
murmured, "Oh, it looks more like an angel than anything.
You must have stayed up all night sewing!"

The dressmaker chuckled softly. "I have two workers who
helped. Mr. Newcomb is making it more than worth my
while, so don't fret. The waist is fine, but the sleeves and hem
look a tad long to me."

She marked them with pins, then said, "Let's slip it off you.
I'll need to have you decide on what lace you like."

Emily carefully skimmed from the dress and looked down
at the frilly petticoats and camisole the seamstress had
brought. She sighed. "I've never worn anything so pretty.
When you had me put these on, I never imagined the dress
could be half as wondrous. Could I just trust you to choose as
you see fit?"

The dressmaker beamed. "Of course."

Someone tapped on the door. Cook went to answer it, then
turned around. "Miss Emily, you're wanted downstairs at
once."

Emily hastily slipped into the fawn-colored dress John
liked so much and stepped into her shoes. She pattered down
the stairs with more speed than decorum, but John never
rushed her, so she figured his summons must be important.
Goodhew met her at the foot of the stairs.

"I'm to take you to the study, Miss." He did just that, then
flashed her a smile and patted her hand as he let go of her arm
and opened the door. "I wish you every happiness."

Puzzled, Emily stepped into the study and into John's waiting arms. He embraced her and whispered in her ear, "I have
an early wedding gift for you, Sweetheart."

Before she could respond, a man said, "Now I've been

waitin' far longer for a hug. Best you step aside, young man."

Emily let out a sharp gasp.

Both of her parents stepped out from behind a bookcase. John didn't let go. He swept her into his arms and laughed loudly as he closed the distance in a few hasty steps. "I'll share her."

ҙ

Emily stood at the back of the church in her beautiful, rustling wedding gown. Her father gave her a kiss and murmured, "He's a good man. He'll keep you happy."

She smiled at her father and nodded. Truer words had not been spoken. Since her parents' arrival, John told her that the very day he'd learned her parents were still alive, he'd sent one of his own vessels clear across the ocean to fetch them. He'd never mentioned a word of it to her, fearing her parents might not be alive or located. That vessel carried food to be left behind, and John ordered it to be filled with those wishing to come to America. Several other families were celebrating reunions due to his kindness.

The organ began to play. It was time to forge a new family of her own. Emily whispered a quick prayer of thanks and let her father lead her to her beloved.

epilogue

Seven years later

"Hurry, Mama."

John swept his six-year-old daughter into his arms and chuckled. "Anna, Mama has her hands full. Be patient."

"The ship is waiting!"

"It's not going anywhere without my say-so," he reassured his daughter. He watched his wife with pride as she threaded her way toward him. They'd become separated in the throng, but that was nothing new. Emily often paused to speak to folks, and they adored her.

"Watch it!" Duncan yanked Timothy and Titus away from the rail. "You know what happens if you fall in!"

John smothered a smile at how both of the youngsters immediately snapped into attention. Emily had planned this whole affair, and the boys knew if they misbehaved, she'd send them back to the house instead of letting them enjoy the picnic. The annual Newcomb Shipping picnic was far too much fun for them to risk banishment.

Emily started the picnic the year they married; and each subsequent year, it turned into a bigger event. It looked as though half of Virginia had turned out for the ship's christening and picnic today. John watched his wife as she deftly handled the social demands as if they were nothing. God's goodness and love shone through her, and everyone responded. She'd been worried she'd not be able to handle high society, but she was their darling. Still, she'd not changed. The lowliest sailor's wife got the same reception as a debutante.

"Nonny, call Mama and tell her to hurry," Anna insisted. "She's your little girl. She has to 'bey you."

Emily's mother turned and fussed with Anna's hair for a moment. "Now, now, our Anna. Mama's letting folks make a fuss over baby Phillip. They've not seen him before. Once she comes on up here, everyone's going to be paying attention to you, so he's getting his turn first."

"Papa, boat!" Lily said gleefully as she hung onto her grandfather's lapel.

"Aye, and a fine one she is."

"Who is fine?" Emily asked as John reached for her hand and helped her up the steps.

"You are, Dear." He smiled at her. "You're magnificent. Ready?"

She nestled a bit closer and rearranged Phillip on her shoulder. "Yes. Everything is perfect."

They exchanged a loving look. They'd discussed names for the ship for months. Only yesterday had they agreed, so John came down to the dock later that day and painted the name on the vessel himself.

Moments later, after John finished praying aloud and asking a blessing on the new ship, he put a bottle in Anna's little hands and helped her swing it. In a clear, high voice, she declared, "I christen thee the *Contentment*!"

A Letter To Our Readers

ar Reader:

In order that we might better contribute to your reading
oyment, we would appreciate your taking a few minutes to
pond to the following questions. We welcome your com-
nts and read each form and letter we receive. When com-
ted, please return to the following:

Rebecca Germany, Fiction Editor
Heartsong Presents
PO Box 719
Uhrichsville, Ohio 44683

Did you enjoy reading *Precious Burdens* by Cathy Marie Hake?
❏ Very much! I would like to see more books by this author!
❏ Moderately. I would have enjoyed it more if

_____

_____

_____

Are you a member of **Heartsong Presents**?   ❏ Yes   ❏ No
If no, where did you purchase this book? _____

_____

How would you rate, on a scale from 1 (poor) to 5 (superior),
the cover design? _____

On a scale from 1 (poor) to 10 (superior), please rate the
following elements.

____ Heroine	____ Plot
____ Hero	____ Inspirational theme
____ Setting	____ Secondary characters

6. How has this book inspired your life?_____
_____
_____

7. What settings would you like to see covered in future
   Heartsong Presents books? _____
_____
_____

8. What are some inspirational themes you would like to see
   treated in future books? _____
_____
_____

9. Would you be interested in reading other **Heartsong
   Presents** titles? ❑ Yes ❑ No

10. Please check your age range:
    ❑ Under 18   ❑ 18-24
    ❑ 25-34   ❑ 35-45
    ❑ 46-55   ❑ Over 55

Name_____
Occupation _____
Address _____
City_____ State_____ Zip_____
E-mail_____

Prairie County Fair

In Prairie Center, Kansas, all of Prairie County gathers *After the Harvest* for its first organized fair, and Judith Timmons hopes it's the last event she has to attend before moving back East.

As Anita Gaines prepares entries for the 1905 fair, she also faces *A Test of Faith*. Will she find the love of her life only to lose him?

Garrison Gaines enters Prairie Center society as a judge at the 1946 fair cook-off. Will he find a *Goodie Goodie* there to benefit his new catering business?

At the fair's "beautiful baby" contest rehearsals, old high school friends Zachary Gaines and Beth Whitrock renew acquaintances. Can a man who has vowed never to marry again have *A Change of Heart*?

Historical, paperback, 336 pages, 5 ³⁄₁₆" x 8"

❤ ❤ ❤ ❤ ❤ ❤ ❤ ❤ ❤ ❤ ❤ ❤ ❤ ❤

❤ ❤ ❤ ❤ ❤ ❤ ❤ ❤ ❤ ❤ ❤ ❤ ❤ ❤

Heartsong

HEARTSONG PRESENTS TITLES AVAILABLE NOW:

------ **Presents** ------

Great Inspirational Romance at a Great Price!

Heartsong Presents books are inspirational romances in contemporary and historical settings, designed to give you an enjoyable, spirit-lifting reading experience. You can choose wonderfully written titles from some of today's best authors like Peggy Darty, Sally Laity, Tracie Peterson, Colleen L. Reece, Debra White Smith, and many others.

When ordering quantities less than twelve, above titles are $3.25 each.
Not all titles may be available at time of order.

JHEARTSONG ❤ PRESENTS

Love Stories
Are Rated G!

That's for godly, gratifying, and of course, great! If you love a thrilling love story but don't appreciate the sordidness of some popular paperback romances, **Heartsong Presents** is for you. In fact, **Heartsong Presents** is the only inspirational romance book club featuring love stories where Christian faith is the primary ingredient in a marriage relationship.

Sign up today to receive your first set of four, never-before-published Christian romances. Send no money now; you will receive a bill with the first shipment. You may cancel at any time without obligation, and if you aren't completely satisfied with any selection, you may return the books for an immediate refund!

Imagine. . .four new romances every four weeks—two historical, two contemporary—with men and women like you who long to meet the one God has chosen as the love of their lives. . .all for the low price of $10.99 postpaid.

To join, simply complete the coupon below and mail to the address provided. **Heartsong Presents** romances are rated G for another reason: They'll arrive Godspeed!